# Tellable Cracker Tales

# Tellable Cracker Tales

Annette J. Bruce

PINEAPPLE PRESS, INC., Sarasota, Florida

Inquiries should be addressed to:
Pineapple Press, Inc.
P.O. Box 3899
Sarasota, Florida 34230-3899


LIBRARY OF CONGRESS
CATALOGING IN PUBLICATION DATA

Bruce, Annette J., 1918-
    Tellable cracker tales / Annette J. Bruce. — 1st ed.
        p.     cm.
    ISBN 1-56164-100-6 (alk. paper)        1-56164-094-8 (pb)
    1. Folklore—Florida 2. Country life—Florida 3. Florida—Social life and
customs. I. Title.
    GR110.F5B78  1996
398'.09759—dc20
                                                                    95-41668
                                                                    CIP


First Edition
10 9 8 7 6 5 4 3 2 1

Design by Carol Tornatore
Printed and bound by Edwards Brothers, Ann Arbor, Michigan

Dedicated to

John, Bette, & Barbara,

who also have sand in

their shoes . . .

# Contents

## Historical Stories

## Tall Tales & Nonsense Stories

## Gator Tales

# Acknowledgments

I wish to express my appreciation to the myriad of storytellers who have, through the years, willingly shared their stories; to the librarians at the Eustis Memorial and Tavares Libraries who are always willing to help me in my search for that evasive answer; and to Linda Chancey of the Bartow Library for going the extra mile to help me in my search. I want to express my gratitude to those who read the manuscript and wrote the preface and blurbs, and to David and June Cussen and the entire staff at Pineapple Press for their enthusiasm and consideration. I want to especially thank my friends Harryette Hannah and Stasia Wiseman for carefully checking the manuscript for typographical errors.

# Preface

nnette Bruce's collection of Florida stories is a treasure trove for tellers and readers. By putting some of her favorite tales in written form, she gives aspiring as well as practicing raconteurs material to draw upon, and she offers all who enjoy local Floridian color hours of entertaining reading. On the following pages, she generously shares a volume of gems.

Tales told today at festivals, school assemblies, and special library programs are frequently borrowed from printed sources, but they seldom return, as told by the tellers, to print. Annette Bruce, one of Florida's best-known storytellers, writes stories with much the same idiom and feeling with which she tells them. With this book, audiences can enjoy her tales in print as well as in live performances. Her written collection is sure to be a welcomed addition to any shelf of Floridiana.

The narratives in this book contain historical facts and engaging fictions artfully woven together with lessons for life, messages about social values, and ample measures of wit. Readers can see how a contemporary tale-teller borrows from history: at times adapting types, motifs, and formulae from often collected and anthologized folktales, and at times using known characters, events, and places to add interest and lend authenticity. Like any folktales, Bruce's stories illuminate the teller's personality and vision as much as they reflect the history and culture from which they spring.

Whether you are a teller or a reader of folktales, I know you will enjoy this collection.

*Ormond H. Loomis*
*Chief, Bureau of Florida Folklife*

# Introduction

**A**s this collection of tellable Cracker tales goes to press, I sense the same joy and pain that enveloped me when my two daughters left for their first days at school. I had a deep appreciation for the availability of a good school, and the satisfaction that, to the best of my ability, I had prepared each of them, both mentally and emotionally, but, as they walked away, a lump formed in my throat and a tear trickled down my cheek. That which had been given to me, I had coddled and enjoyed, but the time had then come to let them launch out toward a wider horizon.

It is said, "The best inheritance you can give your heirs is roots so they can stand, and faith so they can fly." The perfect containers for these substances are stories. Roots will not thrive in the cold, rocky soil of facts and figures. Faith is the end result of demonstrated consistencies. To flourish, both need the warmth and integrity of personalities. Because storytelling speaks in a unifiable language, it not only links tellers and listeners, but also connects the past with the future, and bridges the moats that surround generations and cultures.

The art of storytelling, once an endangered specialty, is now enjoying a revival. Many storytelling workshops and festivals are springing up all over the United States and abroad. Thousands attend the annual National Storytelling Festival held the first full weekend in October in the little town of Jonesborough, Tennessee.

It was at one of these Jonesborough festivals that I first heard the popular teller Doc McConnell say, "You only need two things to be a storyteller — gray hair and hemorrhoids. Gray hair so that you will *look* concerned, and hemorrhoids so that you will *be* concerned." Doc McConnell is a marvelous entertainer with a great sense of humor, and he knows that, in reality, the storyteller also needs the writer's command of words, the painter's love of beauty, the orator's rapport with an audience, and even the actor's flair for drama. But all of these accomplishments are to no avail if the teller has no tellable stories.

Often, after a performance, someone will come up to me and say, "I am a storyteller" or "I would like to be a storyteller. Will you tell me where I can find some good stories to tell?"

Finding and choosing the "good" or right stories is what separates the cream from the whey in the art of storytelling. It is by far the most important and the most difficult task in the art. It is a task that cannot be delegated or accomplished by a "hot tip," but there are a few guidelines to help the novice teller find and choose the right story. The teller will find the mother lode of tellable stories among the folktales. A tellable story is not too complicated, not cluttered with description, has some but not too much dialogue, and has a definite beginning, middle, and ending. Tellers will be wise to choose stories that are between five and fifteen minutes in length and which use the flora and fauna that are familiar to both them and their listeners. But, since the right story has to be one that the teller really likes as well as one that fits his or her pace and "lingo," the right story must be the teller's personal choice.

In finding and learning even one story that is really his or hers, a teller will learn to recite many that will eventually go on the back burner or be discarded altogether. But the bona fide storyteller — one worthy of the title — will have stories and a style that are distinctively his or her own. The teller will lift a story off the printed pages, breathe life into it, and it will become the teller's own story. The teller will enjoy telling the story, and audiences will enjoy hearing it told, over and over again.

For years now, Americans have bought more nonfiction books than fiction, and have clamored for educational programming. In an effort to restore storytelling to the status it once enjoyed, tellers have defined it as an educational instrument. In so doing, they have shortchanged the art. I highly recommend using the art to educate; but to cite the by-products of any art form as a reason for its existence is to reduce the art to a tool — like planting our flower gardens with clover instead of roses. The primary function of storytelling is to entertain.

If a story does not entertain it is worthless — salt that has lost its savor — fit only to be trodden underfoot. So, for whatever reason a story is told, the touchstone, the criterion, the main concern of the teller should first, last, and always be: Will my telling this story entertain my audience?

An entertainer is not necessarily a storyteller, but a storyteller is of necessity an entertainer. People do not choose to do things they do not enjoy. It is only when tellers enjoy telling their stories, and their audiences enjoy hearing the stories, that stories can accomplish their intended missions. It is only when stories entertain that listeners want to hear them again and again, and the facts in the stories become indelible impressions in the listeners' minds.

The stories in this book have met the test of tellable tales. Some were told to me by my parents. Others have been related by friends. Last but not least are the stories that have been suggested by historical nuggets.

In relating these stories, it has been my aim to please, but I have also endeavored to be accurate in all historical and geographical details. Although some of the stories are about real people and actual events, I have been more concerned with the truth in the story than whether or not the story is true.

My hope is that you will enjoy these stories and find them worthy of your best efforts when sharing them with others.

Do Tell!

# Tellable Cracker Tales

# Introduction

# Cracker Jack Tales

**W**e are all indebted to **Richard Chase** for his work in collecting and recording the Jack tales. These folktales continue to give hours of pleasure, both to tellers and to listeners, even though they reflect bygone cultures of the Appalachian and English societies from which they came.

Now, meet the Jack from the polyglot society of the Sunshine State, where the two big classes of people are not the "haves and have-nots," but the Crackers and the Yankees.

A Cracker is likely to be a hybrid, for if a transplant adapts well, he will be considered a Cracker in a few years.

The Yankee is anyone who does not appreciate the values of the natives and who is unfamiliar with the climate, flora, and fauna of the state. To the Cracker, the four-letter-word Yankee is one who is afflicted with the "everything-is-better-where-I-come-from" plague.

While the core of the Cracker Jack stories is deeply rooted in Southern folklore, Cracker Jack is a character I created to personify the humor and values of the typical native Floridians as I have observed them for more than three-quarters of a century.

The Florida Jack, like the Appalachian Jack, is a popular character who can, and usually does, fall into a compost pile and come out smelling like a rose. To his Yankee neighbor, this Jack may seem to be shiftless and, at times, even slightly retarded, but don't you sell him short. . . . Meet Cracker Jack.

Do Tell!

**17**

# Bear Hunting – Cracker-Style

C racker Jack and his pa lived on gators and taters and got most of their hard cash from Yankees. They were good fishing guides; so, not only did they get invited, they got paid, to go fishing in the Yankees' fancy fishing boats.

There was nothing that Jack liked to do any better than to fish except to hunt. But he soon learned that more Yankees came to Florida to fish than came to hunt; so, Jack never missed a chance to talk about the big game that could be found in Florida's scrubs and swamps, and brag about his ability to stalk and kill wild hogs, panthers, and bears.

Much of his talk was only that. In truth, Jack and his pa were not equipped to kill big game, and Cracker Jack would not only give those varmints a wide berth, he was actually afraid of those man–eating critters.

"Jack, son," his pa said one day. "Iffen you don't knock off some of this here big talk 'bout bears and sech, you're gonna talk yoreself into more trouble than you can talk yoreself outten."

But Jack kept it up, and his advertising got results. Three of their best fishing customers came back to Florida and wanted Jack and his pa to take them on a bear hunt.

When Jack named his price, he thought that would make them change their minds, but they readily agreed to the price, and added that if they were successful, they would give Jack and his pa a nice bonus.

Jack and his pa had no thought of getting the bonus, and, under the condition it was offered, did not want it. They just wanted to save their reputation as reliable guides. So they decided to take the Yankees to Emeraldo Island in central Florida where deer and small game were plentiful, but no bears had been seen in years. They arrived at an empty cabin on the island about nightfall and set up camp.

Early the next morning, for the benefit of their Yankee customers, Jack said, "Pa, while you're gettin' breakfast, I'll walk out and size up the situation." He picked up his gun and walked off, grinnin'.

He was ambling along, feeling good about the situation, when out from behind a thicket of palmettos and gallberry bushes stepped one of the biggest, meanest-looking, man-eating bears Jack had ever seen.

Cracker Jack dropped his gun (for he knew it would just be in his way), wheeled around, and started running. He ran and ran until he was hassling and his tongue was hanging out like a hound dog's after a fox chase. He slowed up to catch his breath, but he caught sight of that bear hot on his trail so he took off again. Just when he was about to give up in despair, Jack sighted the cabin. The cabin door was open, and his pa was in the front yard. He got his second wind and made for the open door with the bear gaining on him all the time.

Just as the bear made a lunge for Jack, Jack stumped his toe on the threshold to the cabin and fell. The bear jumped completely over Jack into the cabin. Cracker Jack jumped up, pulled the door closed, latched it, and hollered out, "There's the first one! Y'all kill him and Pa will skin him out while I'm roundin' up the second one."

When the Yankees gave Cracker Jack and his pa their bonus, they said, "Boys, you can expect us back to do some fishing, but don't count on us doing any more bear hunting — Cracker-style!"

**Telling time: 6-7 minutes**
**Audience: middle school - adult**

*Unlike the Appalachian Jack Stories, most Cracker Jack stories are short. Every teller needs several fillers to round out a program. The Cracker Jack stories fill the bill, for they are not only short, but they also bring a chuckle and have a wide appeal. I have found that men are especially fond of the Cracker Jack stories. Remember to keep these stories uncluttered, and do not rush the telling.*

# Sech As It Is

T here was nothing that **Cracker Jack** detested more than clearing new ground. But as sure as Christmas rolled around, the following day the grub hoes would be stacked in front of the tool shed, and one of them would have his name on it.

Jack was now fourteen years old and wanted to be treated like a man, but he was not too anxious to work like one. The hand-blistering, back-kinking job of digging up palmetto roots was not to his liking, to say the least. But Jack's pa was determined that as long as his offspring stayed under his roof and put their feet under his table, they would do his bidding.

In a burst of anger, Jack told his ma, "Clearin' land is work for oxen. It will kill a body before his time. I ain't pickin' up that grub hoe again. I'm leavin' here."

His ma's eyes filled with tears, but she said nothing. But his pa, who overheard Jack's threat, walked into the kitchen and asked, "Do you need any help packin'?"

Jack packed an old saddlebag, and with his Christmas money in his pocket, he headed off on the old mare, Brocade. He had no idea where to go. He ambled over to a cousin's home, a few miles north of Alligator. But his uncle had all his cousins clearing new ground too. So Jack saddled Brocade early the next morning and headed out again. As he pondered on which direction to take, a cold wind, blowing from the northwest, slipped through his clothing and sent chill bumps right down his spine. This took care of his indecision. He turned his back to the wind and headed southeast. All day he rode through the pine woods, and as the sun started setting, he stopped at a little cabin and asked if he could get a night's lodging, something to eat, and some food for his horse.

Brocade was given some corn-nubbins, and Jack did not fare any better. He shared the sowins and gopher-meat which the old woodsman had for his evening meal. As hungry as Jack was, he could hardly get the sowins past his nose, and no amount of chewing could prepare the gopher-meat for swallowing. He didn't sleep well on the pile of moss in the enclosure at one end of the back porch.

But the next day, still wanting to put more distance between him and the grub hoe, Jack rode on. At nightfall, he stopped before another cabin. Again he asked if he could get a night's lodging and something to eat.

The woman replied, "You're welcome, if you can put up with sech as it is."

Although sowins and gopher were again placed before Jack, he satisfied his hunger and slept soundly. He was up with the sun and on his way. He rode to mid-afternoon that day without seeing anyone. When he saw a sorry-looking little cabin surrounded by a rail fence, he was glad, for he was sure that his stomach was rubbing a blister on his backbone, and the old mare seemed tuckered out. Brocade stopped and started nibbling at the wire-grass around the gate post. Jack called out to make his presence known. A worried-looking woman stood up from her squatting position where she was pounding corn. Jack asked if he could get a night's lodging and something to eat.

The woman brushed her lank hair from her wrinkled face and smiled a toothless grin. "Yo're welcome as the sun, iffen ye can stand sech as it is," she said.

Jack thought about his ma's hot biscuits, chicken and dumplings, sweet potatoes, and fresh pork sausage, and he thought about the sowins and gopher-meat which had constituted "sech-as-it-is" since he left home. He thanked the woman, climbed back into the saddle, and turned the mare around.

"Let's go home, Brocade," he said. "No grub hoe has ever been made that will kill a body as quick as these folks' sech-as-it-is."

**Telling time: 8–9 minutes**
**Audience: middle school – adult**

*While it is usually best to give the title and credits after the story, any explanation necessary for the understanding of the story should be made before you start it. You may want to note that "sowins" is a corruption of sourings, a dish made of water added to cracked corn and allowed to sour in the sun. If you are telling to people who are not familiar with Florida fauna, you may want to tell them that a gopher is a vegetarian land tortoise. It burrows into the ground, can live many years, and can become very tough. You might also explain that "Sech as it is" or "such as it is" was a much-used Southern expression. It was used as an apology for the lack of food and as an expression of humility or false modesty when there was an overabundance of food.*

# Successful Cracker Jack

I was by Cracker Jack's home the other day. Jack was not there, but his pa told me to "drag up a chair and sit a spell."

I could tell he was in one of his rare talkative moods, and since I'd never miss the chance to hear him talk, I dragged up that chair. He started telling me about his family. "As you probably know, I have three sons: Tom, Will, and Jack. Jack is the youngest and the only one who's been successful."

I was surprised to hear him say that, because I had heard that both Tom and Will had been off to college. So I said, "No, I didn't know that!"

"Yup, my oldest son, Tom, wanted to be a doctor. So I sold off a tract of land I had close to Kissimmee and sent him off to college, but he didn't make his grades. Came back home, a failure.

"And," he continued, "my second son, Will, wanted to be a preacher. So I sold the turpentine rights offen all my Palatka property and sent him to one of them seminars. He got through there by the skin of his teeth, but he did graduate, and they gave him a church in Apopka. But at the end of the year, they wus the first ones at that convention wantin' themselves a new preacher. So they sent Will to Umatilla, but at the end of that year, there wus a whole bunch of them Umatilla folks campin' on the convention's doorsteps and demandin' a new preacher.

"Then," he continued, "they sent Will over here to Cedar Key. At the end of that year, no complaints at headquarters, and Will, or Reverend William, as he started callin' himself now, stayed on at Cedar Key another year. And even then, none of them Cedar Key folks came to complain.

"I decided to mosey over that way to see if Reverend William had really become a preacher. I didn't tell nobody who I was. I jest went over there and set 'round on the waterfront till an old codger came along, set down, and started talkin'.

"After talkin' a spell, I asked him what he thought of this Reverend William? He told me he liked him jest fine. I was glad to hear that, so I questioned him a little more. 'So this Reverend William is a good preacher?' I asked. 'Oh, I wouldn't go so far as to say that,' he said. 'Ya see, we don't want no preacher here, no how, and Preacher Bill is the nearest to no preacher we ever had.'

"Last week marked the seventh year Will's been in Cedar Key. So you see," continued Jack's pa, "Will is a failure too. But Jack? Jack never did want to be nothin' atall but a lazy, good-for-nothin' Cracker, and he shore is successful."

**Telling time: 5 minutes**
**Audience: adults**

*As you tell this story, keep a mental picture of an old codger, sitting in the shade whittling. He's a slow talker.*

# Introduction

# Folktales & Legends

C racker folktales, like Cracker folks, come from the four corners of the earth. Some tales have been retold by innovative tellers who have refurbished the story with the flora and fauna of Florida, and a few tellers have been able to capture an essence of the varied cultures found in the Sunshine State. The good folktales of the world, in both their old and new dress, are to be found in the repertoire of one or more of Florida's many storytellers. Although the folktales in this volume are not well known, they have been told to, and approved by, discriminating audiences.

Do Tell!

# Judge of Character

I n 1850, central Florida was sparsely settled and schools through-
out the state were few and far between. Often children would go
for months without seeing anyone other than their immediate
family. Their education, for the most part, depended on their mother,
and if she died while they were still young, the children's education was
often ended.

The exception to this was Hiram Perkins. The footprints were still
fresh on his young wife's grave when Hiram decided to do something
about his daughter's education.

"MaryBeth," he said to her one day, "I've invited a friend of yore ma's,
God rest her soul, to come and spend some time with us this winter. He
is a preacher-man and will be able to help you in readin', 'ritin', and
'rithmetic."

"Well, Pa," MaryBeth said, "I'm powerful glad that you done that, but
it kinda bothers me that you asked a preacher to come to stay with us
when I can't cook any better than I can."

"Daughter," Hiram said, "don't you worry about the cookin'. I'll take
care of that. You jest take care of yore other duties, and work on
learnin'."

"I'll do that, Pa."

The day that Brother Livewell was due to arrive, Hiram was up long
before the sun. Out in the backyard he dug a large shallow hole, and
with some lighter wood started a fire in it. When it was burning good,
he added some slow-burning buttonwood. Then he took his gun, went
down to the lake, and killed a couple of nice fat ducks, dressed, and
roasted them.

"Daughter," he called to MaryBeth, "I'm taking the wagon over to Fort Butler to pick up Brother Livewell. When you finish cleaning the kitchen, sweep the porch, dust the parlor, and set the table, but don't you touch those two ducks I've got in the pie safe."

"Yes sir, Pa."

MaryBeth went out to the crib and got a double handful of broom straw, made herself a new broom, swept the porch, and started back to get the duster. That was when she got a good whiff of that mouth-watering aroma of those ducks. She said to herself, "I'll just open the door and take a peek. No harm in that." Oh, they were roasted to perfection. MaryBeth eyed them and started drooling like an old English bulldog. Hmm, she thought to herself, those ducks shore do look good, but sometimes Pa forgets to season things like he should. I'll jest reach under here and get a little taste to see if they need more salt.

Well, those ducks were as good as they looked, and that bite called for another one and another, and by the time she had the parlor dusted and the table set, she had eaten not just one, but both of those ducks. Just when she was finishing off the last one, she heard her pa's wagon coming through the woods. Quickly she grabbed the duck bones, ran out back, and buried them. She rushed back to the house, washed her hands and face, and was on the porch to meet her pa and Brother Livewell.

Hiram, beaming with pride, introduced his daughter to Brother Livewell. "You sure do favor your late mother, God rest her soul," said Brother Livewell.

"Now, daughter," said Hiram, "you take Brother Livewell into the parlor and get acquainted with him while I finish up dinner."

MaryBeth had just got the preacher seated when she heard her pa sharpening a knife on his razor strop, and she knew he would soon be looking for those ducks. She also became painfully aware that he might use that razor strop on her when he didn't find them; so, she began to cry.

"Why, daughter, what's the matter?" asked the preacher.

"It's just too dreadful. I just can't tell you."

"Now, I am here to help any way I can, but you will have to tell me your problems or I can't help you."

"But Pa is so good in most ways. I don't want to tell on him."

"I understand," said the preacher, "but you can tell me."

"Well," sobbed MaryBeth, "please understand, this is his only fault. But it is a bad one!"

"What is it, child?"

"He jest keeps invitin' preachers here."

"What's wrong with that?"

"He always cuts off both of their ears," sobbed MaryBeth.

"What did you say?"

"Yes sir, he always cuts off both of their ears — every preacher who is foolish enough to come here."

"Will you fetch my satchel, Daughter? Never mind, I'll get it myself."

Brother Livewell was out of the yard and down the lane when MaryBeth went to the kitchen and said, "Pa, that preacher-man you brought here has done took both those ducks and is way down the lane with them."

Hiram ran out on the porch and saw the preacher making tracks, fast. "Brother Livewell," he yelled, "where are you going? Come back here!"

Brother Livewell called back over his shoulder, "I'm telling you right now, you old reprobate, you'll not be getting your carving knife anywhere near these two." And he kept on running as fast as he could in the direction of Fort Butler.

Hiram stood there watching until the preacher was out of sight. He shook his head. "MaryBeth, I'm sorry 'bout that. I thought yore ma was a better jedge of character than that."

"So did I," said MaryBeth. And then added, "God rest her soul."

**Telling time: 10-12 minutes**
**Audience: 3rd grade - adult**

*Children relate well to this story, and adults appreciate the historical bits and the story line. It is used by feminists to show the cleverness of the female. At least three cultures — English, Creole, and African — claim this story as their own, with little variation in the telling.*

# Need or Greed

**M**eMa Driggers lived in a ragged old tent that was pitched right smack-dab in the middle of one of the small islands in the Wekiva River. In this ragged old tent, she had a rusty old stove, a rackety old bed, and a rickety old chair — not much of a place to live, for sure! But MeMa was not one to complain — not at all!

Often, she was heard to say, "It's a place to call home, and I'm mighty thankful for it — even if it does leak when it rains."

One day, when MeMa was out picking wild berries for her supper, she saw a large raccoon. Instead of running away from her, the raccoon started walking toward her. This frightened MeMa, and she reached for a stick to defend herself.

The raccoon stopped and spoke. "I didn't mean to frighten you."

"Grinnin' gators!" said MeMa. "A talkin' 'coon! It's not every day that a body sees the likes of that!"

"No, it isn't," said the raccoon. "I thought you might be lonely so I dropped by for a visit."

When MeMa started home, the raccoon went with her, and when they got to her ragged old tent, MeMa invited him in. He went right in, and MeMa fixed him a bowl of berries and herself a cup of tea. Then she sat down in the rickety old chair to continue their visit.

The raccoon finished his berries, licked his lips and said, "MeMa, are you happy?"

"Oh, happy enough, I reckon. I share our president's opinion that most people are as happy as they want to be. But I know I'd be a lot happier if I just had a little cabin to live in."

"You would?" asked the raccoon.

"Oh, yes," declared MeMa.

"Well, hold tight!" said the raccoon, and he covered his eyes with his front paws and yawned a big yawn.

Everything started turning around and around, and when it stopped, MeMa found herself sitting in a nice little cottage.

She rubbed her eyes, and said, "Thank you! Thank you! Thank you! How did you do that?"

But that raccoon was gone! MeMa looked about, and her eyes got as big as lily pads. My! She had a lovely little cottage with nice new furniture. She went to the front door and looked out. Her front yard was neat with manicured flower beds. Out back was a nice vegetable garden with rows of fruit trees, and a little hound dog wagging his tail. MeMa was so pleased.

A few days later she was polishing her new stove when her dog started barking. She went to the door and saw that raccoon in the yard. She quickly called off the dog and invited the raccoon in.

He walked in, looked about, and said, "A nice place you have here."

"Oh, yes," said MeMa. "It is nice! And it would be perfect, if I only had . . ."

"Careful now, MeMa," cautioned the raccoon.

"Oh, I just want some chickens, geese, a horse, and a cow, and a barn to keep them in."

"Is that all?" asked the raccoon.

"Yes, that's all," MeMa assured him.

"Well, hold tight!" said the raccoon, and again he covered his eyes, and yawned. And again everything started going around and around.

When it stopped, MeMa had her chickens, geese, a horse, and a cow, and the barn to keep them in. But MeMa was getting things entirely too easily now. She forgot to thank the raccoon.

Weeks later, MeMa was in her cheerful kitchen, cooking up some guava jelly. She was stirring, tasting, and testing when the raccoon spoke to her from the back screen door.

"How's the jelly?" he asked.

"Oh, I'm so glad you are here," MeMa said, ignoring his question. "There are a number of things I need."

"MeMa," said the raccoon. "I'm disappointed in you. You have become greedy."

MeMa got upset when he accused her of being greedy, spilled hot jelly on her hand, and burned her fingers.

She yelled at the raccoon. "It is not greed! It is need! I need a man to take care of the gardens, animals, and barn, and a woman to cook and keep this house clean."

"Is that all?" asked the raccoon.

"Oh, no!" said MeMa. "I need a ferry, a carriage, some fine clothes, diamond earrings, money to travel, and I want a French Poodle instead of that old hound dog . . ."

"MeMa," the raccoon interrupted. "Some people never know when they are well off!" And with that he covered his eyes and yawned again.

Again everything started going around and around. This time there was wind, rain, hail, thunder, and lightning. When the storm was over, MeMa found that she was sitting in her rickety old chair, under her ragged old tent, with her rackety old bed and her rusty old stove. Everything was just as it was before she met the raccoon, except now, she had burned fingers.

**Telling Time: 10-12 minutes**
**Audience: kindergarten – adult**

*Everyone enjoys this story. It is easy to learn and easy to tell. The much-needed lesson in the story is coated with a bit of magic and should be told in a tongue-in-cheek fashion. The rhythm, repetition, and humor all contribute to the story's success.*

# No Difference

**M**olly was not pretty, neither was she ugly — just an ordinary-looking girl. She was talented, dependable, hard-working, and had patience enough to teach her myna bird, Buddy Boy, to talk.

Molly enjoyed her work as a dancer. She had a small but nice apartment and a dependable car. She should have been happy, but Molly was an overachiever. When someone, posing as her friend, offered her some "fast bucks" to become a link in a smuggling chain, she decided this was her chance to get ahead. She justified breaking the law by convincing herself that everyone broke laws and that she really needed the money.

"Besides," she said, "what I do is like one grain of sand here in Florida — it'll make no difference, no difference at all!" Often, she reassured herself by saying aloud, "No difference, no difference at all!"

She continued her work as a dancer and started making her deliveries. Her savings started growing, and her guilt shrinking. Seldom did she have to say that it made no difference, but now it was Buddy Boy's favorite refrain — "No difference! No difference, at all!"

One morning, Molly awoke feeling strange. She looked into the mirror and discovered that one side of her face was swollen so that it was badly disfigured.

As she took the cover off Buddy Boy's cage and gave him food and fresh water, he kept cocking his head from side to side and calling out, "No difference! No difference, at all!"

"You are wrong, Buddy Boy. This does make a difference. There's no way I can work looking like this. I'll have to call in sick and go to the doctor."

She sought the help of doctor after doctor, but none could find the cause or a cure. Her bank account dwindled. When she was about to give up in despair, she heard of a doctor in Miami who was known for his ability to diagnose strange afflictions.

When the Miami doctor examined her, he said, "This is more than a simple physical ailment, but a number of cases have been cured."

"Good! Give me the prescription, quickly!"

"Not so fast! Not so fast! My fee for this service is high, must be paid in advance, and carries no guarantee."

She wrangled and haggled with him, but he insisted on the last dime of her savings. At last, as she could see no other way out of her dilemma, she gave in and paid him.

When he had his fee, he said, "This illness is usually caused by a wrong the patient has done to mankind. If you are guilty, the only way to be cured is to repent of your misconduct. Then go west of Gainesville to the Devil's Millhopper. Due south of this sinkhole is a large moss-draped oak tree. It is beneath this tree that the sand-elves frolic, beginning at midnight, the first night of the full moon. They like to be entertained. If you dance for them, and they are pleased with your performance, they may grant you a cure. But remember, you must dance your best, as they do not like second-rate entertainment."

This was not what Molly expected or wanted to hear. But she had no other choice but to follow his instructions.

The evening of the full moon, she made her way to the Devil's Millhopper and found the tree. The place gave her the fidgets. She paced the ground and then climbed the tree to hide in the moss and foliage.

At the stroke of midnight, she heard little voices. Looking down, she could see little sand-elves clambering over the rim of the sinkhole like ants over an anthill. Soon she heard music and laughter. She grew so eager to see what was going on that she gave her presence away.

The sand-elves stopped. Molly felt that her heart stopped too. Then one of them called out: "Whoever is in our tree, come down at once, or we must come up and get you."

Molly started climbing down, but she was so nervous that she slipped from the bottom limb and plopped down on the ground in a most awkward manner. She picked herself up, brushed the sand from her jeans and stood there looking and feeling most awkward and foolish.

"Well," said the spokesman, "who are you, and what are you doing here?"

At this point, Molly wondered the same thing, but she got her thoughts together and told them her sad story. She told them how she was a dancer who was now so disfigured that she was unable to work. And explained how she had spent all of her money on doctors and that one had told her to come there to ask them for a cure.

"We will see about that. First, you must dance for us. Should your dancing please us, we may be able to do something, but if you dance poorly, we will punish you for interrupting our frolic-night. Take that warning, and dance away!"

After saying that, he and all the other elves sat in a large ring. Molly had not practiced her dancing in weeks. She was in no mood to perform, but the sand-elves refused to humor her.

"Begin!" shouted their leader, and "Begin! Begin!" shouted the rest in chorus.

In desperation Molly began. She first tried a ballet routine, but that didn't go well. Then she did a clogging step or two from one of her work routines, but her heart was not in it. She flopped down on the ground and said she could dance no more.

The sand-elves were angry. They crowded around her and cried out, "Come here to be cured, indeed! You've come here with one big cheek, but you'll go home with two. Between the two there will be no difference — no difference at all!"

The road home was long for Molly, and she fell into bed. It was noon the next day before she had the courage to look in the mirror. It was true, there was no difference, no difference at all — not between her two cheeks. Both were swollen so she could scarcely see.

Molly was angry with the sand-elves. She was angry with Buddy Boy. She was angry with the world. She was so angry, she was ill.

It was several days before she admitted it was she, not the world, who was out of step. She made up her mind to put her life back in order. She started practicing her dancing. Hour after hour, day after day, she practiced. The next full moon, she made her way back to the Devil's Millhopper. She sat under the sand-elves' frolic-tree. Everything seemed peaceful and in harmony. She became conscious of the myriad of stars twinkling above and the luminous moon bathing the night with splendor. She listened to the night sounds, the murmuring of the breezes and the gurgling of the underground river where it surfaced at the bottom of the sinkhole, and realized just how wrong she had been to think that what she did made no difference. She was remorseful and determined never again to choose to break laws, of man or nature.

Tonight, when the sand-elves came scrambling over the rim of the sinkhole, Molly ran over to the leader. She begged so hard to be given another chance that he gave it to her. This time, when the elves were seated, she did not wait for them to tell her to begin. She started right in with an interpretive ballet of the mockingbird's song, moved into the Charleston with the rhythm of the gurgling sound from the bottom of the sinkhole, and the frogs gave the beat for the clogging routine that brought the sand-elves to their feet.

They clapped their tiny hands and shouted, "Go! Go! Go! Dance more, for we are pleased." And so Molly danced until she dropped to the ground and could dance no more.

Then the leader of the sand-elves said, "We are well pleased and as a reward your face is cured." With these words, the sand-elves vanished.

Molly's way home seemed short. She looked in the mirror and cried with joy to see her face normal again.

When she removed the cover from Buddy Boy's cage, he again cocked his head from one side to the other, calling out, "No difference! No difference at all!"

"Buddy Boy," Molly said, "I have news for you. You are still wrong — very wrong! No matter how ordinary and insignificant a person is, it does make a difference what she does."

**Telling Time: 14-15 minutes**
**Audience: 4th grade – adult**

*Teenagers relate to this story and enjoy it in spite of the presence of the sand elves. the mechanical sound of a talking bird is simple to imitate and adds a bit of authenticity to the story. As a natural wonder Silver Springs, for all its beauty and fame, cannot equal the Devil's Millhopper — a great bowl one hundred feet deep with a rare combination of vegetation growing in it and an underground river surfaced at the bottom. Part of its beauty is the lack of commercialism which also contributes to its obscurity. This story will whet the appetite of those who are interested in exploring romantic and historical Florida.*

# The Christmas Groom

**D**aytona was just a small settlement, and the railroad had not reached Ormond. In fact, it was still known as New Britain Colony when John McCormick was washed out to sea and drowned.

His widow and young daughter Hannah lived on in the sturdy cabin he had built overlooking the Halifax River. Widow McCormick was energetic and resourceful. Who but a woman of her caliber would think of replacing the rusted-out screens with the good corners of worn sheets? The ocean breezes came through them, and the insects did not. It did limit their view of the outside, but they didn't spend much time inside the cabin during the day.

Hannah was beautiful in body and spirit. She and her mother were greatly admired and loved by all who knew them, and the folks in the settlement of Daytona were proud to claim them as their own, even though the McCormick cabin was a good ways down the river.

At the close of every war, Florida gets an influx of people, including drifters, and the Civil War was no exception. Among them was Sneaky Sam, a man with a title he had earned. He had only been in Daytona a few days when he saw the most beautiful girl he had ever seen. She was selling Christmas greenery, herbs, and spices. On inquiry, he learned that she was the unwed daughter of the widow McCormick, and, right then and there, he decided that, come what may, he was going to have that beauty as his own. That evening Sneaky Sam "borrowed" a small boat and drifted down the river to the McCormick cabin. He heard someone talking, and he stopped to listen. The voice was coming from the cabin and seemed to be that of the widow McCormick as she prayed.

After lengthy supplications for all the sick and afflicted, Sneaky Sam heard her say, "Dear God and Lord of all, my needs are few. You have graciously provided our daily bread, for which we are thankful, and although you saw fit to take John, you have given me a loving and good daughter. She has been a balm to my soul, but I am now growing old, and I would ask of you, Dear Lord, send a man who will love and provide for her."

Sneaky Sam was not slow in seizing this opportunity. Quickly he hid in an empty rain barrel which was close by the window and, in as deep and awesome a voice as he could muster, said, "Widow McCormick, my good and faithful servant, I have seen your good works and heard your prayers. I am going to reward you accordingly.

"On Christmas day, a man driving a white horse will come for your faithful daughter. Prepare for his coming and accept him as a gift from me, for I have chosen him to be her husband."

The McCormicks were ecstatic; God had spoken to them. But there was no time to go into the settlement to share the news. The days before Christmas were few and must be filled with cleaning, cooking, decorating, and planning, for God's chosen was to be their guest, come Christmas day.

As for Sneaky Sam, he felt pleased with his plan, except that he didn't own a white horse and didn't know where he could borrow one. He felt like kicking himself for being so specific. But, he was not to be outdone. When all other resources were exhausted, he got up early Christmas morning and whitewashed his old nag, borrowed a buckboard, and then, dressed in some borrowed clothes, he made his way out to the McCormick cabin. There he accepted their gracious hospitality in true con-man style.

Hannah was filled with disappointment, misgivings, and fears. This made her feel that she was being an ingrate, and she begged God to forgive her.

Sneaky Sam, not wanting to linger, announced that he had been sent by God to take Hannah as his own. And when Widow McCormick offered to send for the parson to perform the marriage rites, he scoffed at the idea. "Why should mere man mumble words for our union. We are married in God's sight so what more need we ask?"

Widow McCormick was a prudent woman, and found it difficult to accept Sam and his arrangements at face value, but she consoled herself with the assurance that God does work in great and mysterious ways. She set about gathering up things to help them set up housekeeping. Everything was packed into a large, strong chest made of bamboo which Hannah's father had found washed up on the beach the day she was born.

When the chest was loaded on the back of the buckboard, Hannah kissed her mother and climbed aboard.

Sneaky Sam, feeling that his much-desired prize was in his hands, rushed his old horse. It was a warm, humid day and the old nag started to sweat — something Sneaky Sam had not bargained for — and the sweat started removing the whitewash.

Hannah was quiet, but Sneaky Sam knew she was no one's fool. He also knew the high esteem in which the folks in the settlement held Hannah and her mother. He became aware that if she screamed "foul, " those people would "tar and feather" him and ride him out of the country on a greased pole. He thought about the dirty little tumbled-down, lean-to shack he was taking her to, and decided he'd better make some different arrangements.

"My darling Hannah," he said, "I have a gift for you. A very special gift. I want you to close your eyes while I give it to you."

Hannah closed her eyes.

"It is so important that you have your eyes closed when I give you this gift, and you may forget and open them. Here, let me take these things out of this chest, and you get in there."

Obediently, Hannah climbed into the chest. Quickly, Sam closed and locked the lid, pulled the chest off the buckboard and, leaving Hannah locked in the chest at the edge of the trail, rushed into the settlement to take care of the details he deemed necessary. He went by the general store and bought nails and a lock. He went to the shack and nailed up the back door and both windows. He climbed up on a nail keg and put the lock high on the inside of the front door. He returned the borrowed clothes and spread the word all around that he was bringing his bride home and that "like most women, she is a little excitable, and may get carried away, and even scream, but she will calm down in a day or two. So, if you will, just be a good neighbor, and turn a deaf ear to any noise you hear coming from my place."

While Sam was making his last-minute arrangements, a nobleman, by birth and character, was returning to St. Augustine with his hunting party and a Florida panther they had captured. He saw the deserted bamboo chest and asked one of his servants to open it. When the young nobleman saw the beautiful Hannah, he rubbed his eyes, for he was sure he must be looking at an angel. When Hannah saw the handsome hunter, seated on his beautiful white steed, she thanked God for keeping his promise. She told the nobleman how Sneaky Sam had come as a wolf in sheep's clothing.

"The man should be duly rewarded for his efforts," said the nobleman, who then told his servants to put the Florida panther from the cage into the bamboo chest and close and re-lock the lid.

The nobleman took Hannah back to her home, where they were properly married. The nobleman said that he would not think of leaving the widow McCormick there alone; that she must go with them so he could properly protect and care for her. It was a tired but happy wedding party that arrived in St. Augustine, where they lived happily ever after.

And Sneaky Sam? He went back and retrieved the bamboo chest. It was dark when he arrived at his place. He dragged the chest in, climbed up and locked the door, then kicked the keg to one side. He then made his way, in the dark, to the chest, and unlocked the lid. The neighbors did hear some scary screams, and even some pleas for help, which sounded more like a man than a woman, but being good neighbors, they honored Sam's request. They smirked and smiled, but turned a deaf ear to the noise coming from Sam's place.

**Telling time: 15 minutes**
**Audience: 3rd grade – great, great grandparents**

*Although this story smacks of a fairy tale, it is thoroughly enjoyed by adult men and women — anyone who enjoys hearing how a cheater gets what he deserves.*

# The Boot

he owl is often misquoted as asking the question "Who?" The next time you hear an owl, listen carefully and note that he is making the statement, "It's true!" For once, deep in the Everglades, where the wild beasts lived, there lay a man's boot. How it came to be there is hard to say, for no man had ever been there; at least, the beasts there had never seen one. But there was the boot, and when the beasts saw it, they all gathered round to find out what it was. Such a thing was new to them, but they were all ready to show off their wisdom with an explanation.

"Well, I say, there's no doubt what it is," said the bear.

"Oh, of course not," said the panther, and the alligator, and all the beasts and birds.

"Why, there is no doubt," continued the bear, "that it is the rind of some kind of fruit from a tree. The fruit of the cork tree, I should say. This is cork. It is plain to see," and he showed the sole of the boot.

"Oh! Just hear him!" laughed the raccoon.

"Yeah, just hear him!" cried all the beasts and birds.

"It's not that at all!" said the panther with a glance of scorn at the bear. "Anyone with an iota of common sense would know that it is some kind of nest. Look! Here is the hole for the bird to go in, and here is the deep part for the eggs and young ones to be safe. No doubt at all, I would say!"

"My friend," said the raccoon, "while there is some reason for your conclusion, it is plain to me that a nest it was never meant to be."

"I should say not," shouted the birds. "It is not that at all."

"I should think not," cried the alligator, as he pushed aside the sawgrass to get in a more prestigious position. "It is plain to me that it is some kind of plant. Look at this long root," and he showed the lace at

**41**

the side of the boot. "This is the root of a plant. There's no doubt about it! It is a plant!"

"Not at all!" cried the panther and the bear.

"A plant, I know," declared the deer, who had had little to say, "and a plant it is not!"

All the birds and beasts again chimed in. "No plant!" "No plant at all!" "Why we can see!" "A root? Never!"

"If I might speak," said an old owl, who sat in a tree. "I can tell you what it is. For I have been in a land where there are more of such things than you can count. It is a man's boot."

"A what?" cried all the beasts and birds. "What is a man?" "And what is a boot?"

"A man," said the owl, "well, a man is an animal with two legs, that can walk, run, eat, and talk as we can, but he can do much more than we can."

"Pooh! Pooh! What a ridiculous lie," said the turtle, and pulled his head back into his shell.

"That can't be true!" said the beasts. "How can an animal with only two legs do more than we can who have four? It is false, to be sure."

"Of course it is, if they have no wings," said the birds.

"Well," answered the owl. "They have no wings, and yet, it is true. They can make things like this, and they call them boots, and wear them on their feet."

"Well, that last statement made a firm disbeliever of me," said the opossum.

Then all the birds and beasts cried out, "How do you expect us to believe such an outrageous tale?"

"Such a stupid lie!" screamed the panther.

"Can do more than we can, humph!" growled the bear.

"Wear such things on their feet? How ridiculous!" grunted the alligator.

"Not true! Not true!" they all cried. "It is obvious that what you say is not true. We weren't born yesterday, and we're nobody's fools, and we know what you say is not true! We know that such things are not worn on the feet!"

"Of course, they could not be!" cried the panther.

"It is completely false!" said the bear.

"It is false," cried all the birds and beasts. "Owl, what you say cannot be true! You have knowingly told us a stupid lie; therefore, you are no longer fit to live among us." And they chased the owl from the Everglades.

"It's true! It's true!" said the owl as he flew away, and he still declares it to be so, both in and out of the Everglades.

**Telling time: 8–9 minutes**
**Audience: kindergarten – 4th grade**

*For the teller who can do character voices well this story is a "keeper." It is short, full of action, and if told well will delight children of any age.*

# Sam's Whistle

I t **was during** the second Spanish occupation that Señor Pedro de Ovando arrived in La Florida. He brought with him his comely wife and his beautiful daughter Carmelita. Both the señora and the señorita were so personable that to know them was to love them, but Señor Pedro was pompous, arrogant, overbearing, and could hardly be tolerated. But as the saying goes, we should give even the devil his dues so I must tell you that Señor Pedro was a faithful husband and a concerned father.

When Señorita Carmelita became ill, Señor Pedro summoned the local doctor. When he failed to diagnose the illness, Señor Pedro sent to Cuba and Mexico for medical help. Still she grew thinner, and the blush faded from her cheeks. Señor Pedro, then, risked invoking the wrath of the Council of the Indies and the King of Spain by seeking help in the United States. But it was an old Indian who diagnosed her illness and said that mangoes would cure her.

Señorita Carmelita did not like the mangoes in San Augustin and would not eat them — complaining that they were hard, stringy, and tasted like turpentine. Señor Pedro sent out a proclamation that whoever brought edible mangoes to the señorita would be richly rewarded.

Near San Augustin lived a miller who had, in addition to his mill, three sons, two fine horses, and a donkey. The youngest son, Mark, was the darling of his father's eye. He was so handsome that it was a foregone conclusion that he would marry well. He was never taught a trade or expected to do his share of the work at the mill. He was only encouraged to enhance and preserve his appearance.

John, the second son, was so witty that his father was sure he could demand a good dowry from his wife so he was allowed to spend his time reading and sharpening his wit.

Samuel, the oldest brother, operated the mill, which he was to inherit. Of course, from its profits he was to pay half of its worth to Mark, and half of its worth to John. Yet every day, his father would say, "Sam, operate the mill with care, for it will be yours some day."

Near the mill grew a large mango tree that bore the most delectable mangoes — sweet, fleshy, and flavorful.

When the miller heard of the nobleman's plea, he said to Mark, "Son, get spiffed up in your new suit, while I saddle up the white steed and fill this fine split-oak basket with our best mangoes for you to take to San Augustin.  Hurry along, for no doubt this is your chance to improve your station in life by marrying the beautiful señorita."

Mark was on his way to San Augustin when he met an old hag carrying a crying child. The woman's hair was matted, and her eyes were squinted. She was snaggle-toothed and as wrinkled as a dried prune. The child, which she had slung on her hip, was dirty, and flies were swarming about her face. Mark didn't want to look at them, but they were in his path.

"Young man," cried the old woman, "where are ye goin'?"

"Get out of my way, old woman, and don't bother me with your questions, for it's none of your business where I'm going."

"I see ye don't act as good as ye look. What's that ye got in that basket?"

"Oyster shells," answered Mark. He smirked, and said to himself, not even my witty brother could have come up with a better answer than that.

"Then let it be oyster shells," cried the old woman.

Mark rode on. He arrived in San Augustin, and there he presented his gift to Señor Pedro, who was impressed by Mark's appearance, but when he opened the basket he found it full of old dirty oyster shells. Señor Pedro was furious, and had Mark thrown into the dungeon at the Castillo de San Marcos.

When Mark did not return, the miller told his second son, "John, somehow your brother Mark has not succeeded, but you, with your sharp wit, may well overcome where he failed, so fill the other basket with fruit, and take the dapple mare, and go to San Augustin."

John soon met the same old woman carrying the crying child.

"Good day to ye! Where ye be agoin'?" the old woman asked.

"Old woman, your curiosity is making a fool of you, for it's none of your business where I'm going," replied John.

"Oh, a smart aleck, huh? What ye got in that basket?"

"Coquina rocks," replied John.

"Then rocks let it be," said the old woman.

When John arrived at the San Augustin mansion, he bowed low, and with a sweep of his hat said, "For the health of God's gift to man," and handed the nobleman the basket.

Señor Pedro accepted it with as much pomp as it was offered, but when he opened it, and found rocks, he went into a rage and had John thrown into the dungeon with his brother.

When neither of the boys returned, the miller lost his zest for living. He left all the work for Sam to do. His appetite failed, and he grew feeble. One day, he was surprised to see Sam gathering a sack of the blushing mangoes.

"What are you doing?" he asked.

"Picking some mangoes for the ill señorita," Sam replied.

"No, you mustn't go. You can never succeed if both Mark and John have failed. I can neither spare you nor afford to lose the donkey."

"Pa, I've been doing Mark and John's work for years, and as for the donkey, keep it! I'll walk."

Sam threw the sack of mangoes over his shoulder and started out. He walked until he was hot and tired. When he stopped to rest, he saw the old woman carrying the dirty, crying child.

"Good day to ye, and where might ye be agoin'?" she asked.

"Good day to you, fellow traveler. I'm going to San Augustin, and to where are you traveling?" answered Sam with a smile.

"I'm on my way. What is that ye have in your poke?"

"The best mangoes in the world, which I hope will heal the Señorita Carmelita." Then he reached into the bag and brought out one of the delicious smelling mangoes and handed it to the child. "Here, maybe this one will make you feel better."

The child stopped crying and smiled. The old woman said, "Bless you, my son. Let the mangoes be healing fruit, and for the one you gave to this child, ask what you will, and it will be given to you."

Sam's feet and back hurt so he said, "I'd like to have a whistle that would call to me any animal that I wanted."

The old woman reached deep in her pocket and brought out a silver whistle on a royal blue cord, and said, "Here you are." Then, she and the child disappeared like a wisp of morning fog.

Sam put the whistle to his lips and blew, and up trotted a fine pony.

Sam made a halter from the top part of the burlap sack, and reins from wild vines growing close by.

When Sam arrived in San Augustin, Señor Pedro was unfavorably impressed with Sam, but delighted with the appearance and the aroma of the fruit. Señorita Carmelita ate one of the mangoes, then she ate another, and another, and would have eaten more if her duenna had not stopped her. In a few days the color came back to her cheeks, and she laughed again.

Señor Pedro was ecstatic. He called Sam and asked him what he wanted as a reward. Sam told him he wanted his two brothers. When they were set free, Sam sent them home to run the mill.

Then, he put his silver whistle to his lips, and called up a big, green, slimy, scaly, ug-g-gly alligator, which he brought before Señor Pedro. "Sir," he said, "put your mark on this wild beast and set him free, and a year from today, I will return and call him back as a hallmark of honesty between two honorable gentlemen."

Señor Pedro, still in a most appreciative mood for his daughter's health, laughed and said, "There is no way that you can call this wild alligator back once you have set him free, but as you have requested, I will mark him, and in a year, if you can call him back, you may have the señorita to wed."

Samuel traveled about for a full year, using his whistle to help people who were in need.

As the appointed day approached, Señor Pedro became apprehensive. Just supposing that peasant should return and somehow capture that alligator. No, no, he didn't want to think of such a thing. It would be too humiliating to have his beautiful daughter marry that peasant. On the appointed day he arose early and walked out on his balcony. He looked down Market Street, rubbed his eyes, and looked again. Then, he rubbed his eyes again, for he could not believe what he was seeing. But there, at this early hour, was Sam, with the alligator walking beside him. Señor Pedro could distinguish his mark from where he stood.

He called to the treasurer, "Quick, go down there and pay whatever you have to to get that alligator from that man and drive it back into the river."

The treasurer paid Sam one hundred pesos for the alligator, but as soon as he goaded it into the Matanzas River, Sam whistled it back. When Señor Pedro saw what happened, he sent the accountant to get the alligator. Sam charged him two hundred pesos. Even though the accountant drove the alligator much further up the river, Sam whistled it back.

The nobleman was now so agitated, he overlooked propriety, and sent his daughter Carmelita to wheedle the alligator from the peasant.

Carmelita talked with Sam and found him to be a pleasant fellow. He was strong and kind, and not the least bit pretentious. But even she was unable to get the alligator from him.

"If your father wants this alligator, he must deal with me directly. Tell him I will be waiting for him back of the pomegranate tree in his garden."

When the señor went to the garden, Sam said, "Señor, you may have the alligator for nothing if you will only kiss it."

The Señor was furious — kiss that loathsome creature? Never! But what else could he do? He looked around to see if anyone else would see him, and when he felt sure no one else would ever know, he kissed that big, green, scaly, slimy, ug-g-gly gator, right where Sam pointed.

Sam then followed the nobleman back inside, and asked, "You will keep your promise? Yes? I marry the Señorita Carmelita?"

What an abominable thought! But how was he going to escape his promise? His displeasure registered on his face, and a member of the junta whispered in his ear, "Tell him to take a sack and travel around the world, and fill it with truth."

The señor told Sam, this he would have to do in order to marry the señorita.

"Good!" said Sam. "Give me the sack." He was given a large sack, and Sam spread the mouth of it, as a miller could, then he said, "There is no need to travel to find truth. There is plenty right here to fill the sack. Señor Pedro, is it not true that I brought you a bag of the best mangoes you've ever tasted?"

"It is."

"Truth go into the sack!" And he made a motion as if he were throwing an item into the sack. "Is it not true that this fruit delighted Señorita Carmelita?"

"It is."

"Truth go into the sack! And is it not true that these mangoes restored the señorita's health?"

"It is."

"Truth go into the sack. And is it not true that I asked you to mark an alligator as a sign of honesty between two men of honor?"

"It is."

"Truth go into the sack. Is it not true that you put your mark on it, and freed it?"

"It is."

"Truth go into the sack. And Señor, is it not true that you promised that I could marry the Señorita Carmelita after a year if I called back the alligator?"

"Well, yes."

"Truth go into the sack. And Señor, is it not true that to get the alligator from me you . . ."

"Stop!" said Señor Pedro. "The sack is full of truth."

"And I marry the señorita?"

"Yes."

It was a garden wedding. The ceremony was performed under the pomegranate tree. Carmelita carried mango blossoms, and Samuel wore the silver whistle around his neck.

**Telling time: 25–26 minutes**
**Audience: 4th grade – adult**

*This version of an old folktale has a Hispanic flavor and will be greatly enhanced if the teller is familiar with the Spanish language and culture. The dramatic teller can prove his mettle with the courtroom scene.*

# Introduction
# Historical Stories

I n history books, Florida is often upstaged by her sister states. Yet in no other state can one find more romance and adventure than can be found on the Florida frontier with its long history as a cow country, its 8,462 miles of tidal coast, its 30,000-plus lakes, and its unique Everglades.

Florida's most celebrated folk hero was Morgan Bonapart Mizell, known to his peers as "Bone." Bone was a cowboy, or cow hunter as they were more often referred to in Florida. He was a celebrated legend in his time, and the center of attention wherever he went.

Jacob Summerlin, the first white child born in Florida after Spain ceded the territory to the United States, was a picturesque cow hunter. The stories of his life will warm the heart and give a chuckle.

Little is known about Orlando Reeves except that he died in the line of duty during the Seminole Wars. His grave was marked with a primitive marker for many years, but now the location of it is not certain.

James Mitchell Johnson was a giant of a man in his day, and accomplished astounding feats, as did the four female giants.

Although the stories in this section are about real people, and are laced with historical facts, they are not intended to supplant the uninteresting history books which gather dust on library shelves. These stories are designed for telling to entertain and educate — with the emphasis on entertainment.

Do Tell!

# The Barefoot Mailman

J ames Mitchell Johnson had a good understanding. He wore a
size sixteen shoe, and even with that much turned under for feet,
he still stood six feet, seven inches tall. Because of the size of his
feet, and the great length of his stride, he was known as "Acre-Foot."

Acre-Foot was born near Lake City in 1847. He grew up during a
time when the entire country was wallowing in an extreme depression.
Florida was especially hard hit because of the Seminole Wars being
fought here. Acre-Foot could and would do the work of two men. Even
so, he found it difficult to find a job. When he was twenty-one, he heard
that the Army planned to string a telegraph line between the forts located along Peace River. Acre-Foot packed up and moved to Fort Ogden
hoping to find work.

The clearing which was made while stringing the telegraph wire was
known as "wire-road." Even with this clearing, it was almost impossible
to get a horse through the Everglades south of Fort Ogden. Official
communications could be sent over the wire, but the regular mail needed to be delivered.

Acre-Foot was thirty years old when an agent from the Post Office
department came to Fort Mead to hire a mail-carrier for the route
between Fort Mead and Fort Myers. Several applicants were already
there when Acre-Foot arrived at the quartermaster's store. Among them
was "Big-Ed" Donaldson, an Army veteran with a loud mouth and a
reputation for being a fighter.

"I'll take the mail down and bring it back once a week," Big-Ed said
in a booming voice. "And I'll guarantee that no matter whut — gators,
rattlesnakes, moccasins, hurricanes, or robbers — it'll go through."

The agent squared his shoulders and smiled. "That's the spirit which
has built the postal service into what it is today."

Acre-Foot stood nearby, but said nothing. When the agent told Big-Ed to sign on the bottom line, Acre-Foot spoke up: "Hold on there just a minute. If ol' Ed can make that trip with a load of mail once a week, I'll go so far as to wager I can make it at least twice a week — maybe three times."

Big-Ed's face flushed with anger, and he roared, "Whut makes you think yore a better man than me?"

Acre-Foot smoothed his mustache. "I ain't a-sayin' I'm a better man, but I am sayin' I'm a better walker, and for shore, the best man for the job."

The two almost came to blows before the agent stopped them. "Come, let's settle this like gentlemen. The man who can walk the fastest will get the job."

Monday morning, the two men stood just inside the gate at the fort. They listened as the postal agent stated that the man who made the most trips to Fort Myers and back that week would be awarded the contract. The agent then fired the starting pistol, and both men moved off.

Quickly Acre-Foot moved out of sight.  He reached Fort Myers just at dusk the same day, and found everyone at the fort busy.

"What's going on?" Acre-Foot asked the soldier at the gate.

"Can it be you don't know?" The sentry asked. "Why, we've done got ourselves a new mail service 'twixt here and Fort Mead, and we're going to hold a big shindig for the carrier when he gets here. Actually, there's two of 'em this trip — some kind of a race. They may get here tomorrow, but more'n likely it'll be the next day."

"Is that right?" said Acre-Foot. "Where's the post office from here?"

When Acre-Foot gave the mail pouch to the postmaster, the fireworks started. The soldiers and settlers around the fort began a celebration, and Acre-Foot showed his appreciation by taking part. He called every square dance except two, and filled in for the fiddler for those.

Early the next morning, Acre-Foot picked up his mail pouch and started out along the wire-road back to Fort Mead. He stopped for a drink of water at Arcadia crossroads. There he saw Big-Ed.

"Well, looks like I've done caught up with you," Big-Ed said, grinning.

"Yep, sure looks like you have," Acre-Foot drawled. "'Cept I'm goin' t'other way."

Acre-Foot Johnson got the contract. He liked the work, but the job only paid twenty-six dollars per month. That would not keep him in shoes, so he walked the treacherous trail six days each week, barefoot.

With such a demanding job, how Acre-Foot found the energy and time to do any romancing is a mystery. But true to his nature, Acre-Foot accomplished the seemingly impossible. He got married, but then he was confronted by another obstacle — how two people could live off his meager earnings. One day, he came up with an idea to make more money. He decided to begin the first passenger service from Bartow to Fort Myers. He built himself an armchair and fitted it with shoulder straps. Just as he was finishing the contraption, a neighbor happened by.

He looked and then he looked again. "What in the world is that?"

"Well, it's like this," Acre-Foot said. "I've got myself a good woman, and we want to raise a family. But I'll have to make more money than I'm making on the mail route so I've decided to take a passenger along with the mail."

"Why, you can't do that!" The neighbor said. "Not many horses can carry a man that far through that swamp."

"I've been making better time than two horses," Acre-Foot replied. "Get in this chair, and I'll show you."

Acre-Foot slipped the straps over his broad shoulders and squatted so the neighbor could get into the chair. Then he took off along the wire-road. After he had gone two or three miles in his long stride, he whirled around and headed back home. When they arrived, the neighbor jumped to the ground and noticed that Acre-Foot was not winded or tired.

"Rides better than a horse," the neighbor said. "Maybe I will ride down to Fort Myers on your back, some day."

"Be glad to have you, any day you want. Just let me know," Acre-Foot said.

Well, it looked as if Acre-Foot had found a way to make the extra money he needed, but the Post Office department foiled his hopes. They refused to allow any of their carriers to take passengers.

Acre-Foot was now making more money with his passenger trade than the postal service was paying him. So, after seven years of faithful service as a mail carrier, he turned in his resignation.

His unique business served him well for about a year, but in 1885 the railroad made both the walking mail route and Acre-Foot's passenger service things of the past.

**Telling time: 15-16 minutes**
**Audience: 4th grade - adult**

*James Mitchell Johnson was a real person who accomplished many super feats, accounts of which have been told and retold with each teller making the story a little better than the one before, until some of the stories have gone beyond belief. I found more than one account of Johnson walking from Ft. Meade (near Bartow) to Fort Myers in one day. It makes a good story, but I find it hard to believe. A recent conversation with a native of that part of the state revealed that while his mail route ran from Ft. Meade to Ft. Myers, he walked from Ft. Meade to Ft. Ogden in one day and on to Ft. Myers the next. That would be difficult to do, but could be done by a man with super stamina and a long walking stride.*

# "Bone" Mizell

n Pioneer Park, at Zolfo Springs, there is a historical marker for Bone Mizell. Bill Bevis, the chairman of the Florida Public Service Commission, in his dedication speech described Bone as being the hardest working, the hardest playing, and the most colorful cowboy the state has ever known.

The historical marker reads: *"Bone" Mizell was DeSoto County's wag, prairie philosopher, cowboy humorist and prankster. He was beloved for his merrymaking. Bone was christened Morgan Bonapart Mizell. He was born 1863 and died 1921. Bone is buried in Joshua Creek Cemetery, in DeSoto County near Arcadia.*

Bone was a topnotch cowboy, but he had only enough schooling to sign his name, and his only clout was his popularity. Yet he was never intimidated by friend or foe, rich or poor, officers of the law or outlaws.

Once a friend of Bone's was arrested for butchering a cow of questionable ownership. When he expressed to Bone his concern about the outcome of the trial, Bone said, "You buy me a John B. Stetson hat, and I'll get you out of this in two minutes."

"How?" asked the friend.

"Just have them call me as a witness."

At the trial, a number of witnesses were questioned about brands and other facts concerning the case. When Bone was put on the stand, he testified that he had seen the alleged butchering. When he was asked where he was at the time he answered, "Bee Branch."

"Where is Bee Branch?" asked the prosecutor. "Everybody knows where Bee Branch is. It's two or three hundred yards over in the next county," answered Bone.

The defense called for a dismissal on the grounds that his client could not be tried in Arcadia for an offense committed in an adjoining county. The case was thrown out of court, and Bone got his hat.

Bone was proud of his new hat, and walked into a courtroom with it on. He was promptly fined twenty dollars by the judge. Bone took a twenty-dollar bill from his pocket and laid it in front of the judge. Then he reached in his pocket, took out another one, and said, "Judge, you better take forty, sir, 'cause I walked in here with my hat on, and I'm gonna walk out the same way."

When the sheriff of DeSoto County was advised of a poker game going on at a nearby ranch, he went to investigate. He found some well-known cattle owners and Bone, cards in hand, sitting around the table with poker chips.

"Boys," the sheriff said, "I'm going to have to pull this game."

"But Sheriff," said one of the players, "we are not playing for money. We're just playing for poker chips."

"Chips are the same as money," the sheriff replied.

The next day, each of the card players was fined eighty-five dollars. Bone waited until the others had paid their fines, then he sauntered up and carefully counted out eighty-five dollars in poker chips.

"Wait a minute," said the sheriff. "This ain't money."

"Sheriff, only yesterday, in front of several witnesses, you said, 'chips are the same as money,'" Bone said, and he turned, and walked out.

Although Bone was not educated, he was no one's fool. A confidence man came to town and set up a table at the county fair. He began hawking ten-dollar shares of stock in a company producing a new universal solvent. In convincing terms he told how the investment would make a fortune for the shareholders in a few years.

From the rear of the crowd, Bone shouted out, "What's a universal solvent?"

"Brother, I'm glad you asked that," the con man replied. "A universal solvent is a liquid that will dissolve anything it touches. Just think of the many uses such a product has . . ."

"Hold on there!" Bone interrupted. "What I want to know is, what're you going to keep this universal solvent in when you get it made?"

Once when Bone was on a cattle drive, his horse gave out. He saw an elderly man plowing nearby, and told the cowboys with him that he was going to trade horses. The cowboys told Bone that the plow horse looked better than his horse, and he would need some cash to make the trade. Bone rode over to the farmer anyway. The cowboys watched from a distance. After a short conversation, they saw Bone pull out a scrap of paper and a stub of a pencil. He scribbled something on the paper and handed it to the farmer. Then they exchanged horses. When Bone returned to the herd with his new mount, one of the cowhands asked him how he made the deal without any money.

"Well, I gave him a promissory note," Bone explained.

"Why Bone, you can't read or write," said one of the cowboys.

Bone just smiled and replied, "Well, he couldn't either."

The crowning stunt of Bone Mizell's life was written in rhyme by Ruby Carson, put to music by Jim Bob Tinsley, recorded by The Drifters, and sung by many balladeers.

This is the "Ballad of Bone Mizell," as it appeared in the 1939 February-March issue of *The Florida Teacher*:

At Kissimmee they tell of old M. Bone Mizell
    And the stranger who died on his hands:
How he died in dry season, and that was the reason
    He was buried awhile on Bone's lands.
He was buried awhile on that pine and palm isle
    In a swamp under Florida's sun
By the Cracker who nursed him, who loved him and cursed him
    Just before his demise had begun.
"Jes take this news ca'mly," Bone wrote to the family
    The deceased had left livin' up north,
"I can send the remains when there come up some rains
    And us pine island folk can go forth.
"So providin' yuh ask it, I'll dig up th' casket"
    Which was done when the season brought rain,
And the river could float the flat-bottomed boat
    And the dead boy could travel again.
When Bone went with the coffin, he smiled much too of'en,
    On the boat and en route to the car.
At the train he said, "Gimme one fare from Kissimmee
    To Vermont! Ain't this corpse goin' far?"
Thus the money was spent that the family had sent.
    And a friend of Bone's said the next day:
"So yuh shipped that lad hum?" And Bone said, "No, by gum
    For I thought hit all over this way:
"As his kinfolks air strangers to all of us rangers,
    Why not give some dead Cracker this ride?

Why not make all this fuss over some pore ole cuss
　　Who in life hadn't wallered in pride?
So instead of that Yank with his money and rank
　　Who had been 'round and seen lots of fun,
I jes' dug up Bill Redd and I sent him instead
　　For ole Bill hadn't traveled 'round none."

As the saying goes — What goes around, comes around. Bone's grave, in the Joshua Creek Cemetery, remained unmarked for over thirty years before some of his friends decided to donate a tombstone for his final resting place, and don't you know, the small inscribed marker was placed on the wrong grave!

Bone was a hard-working and hard-playing cow hunter, and to his detriment, he was also a hard drinker. Once he told a friend, "Some day when I'm about eighty-five, they'll find me dead, and everybody will say, 'Well, old Bone's dead, and liquor killed him.'"

He was right on target, except for his age. Instead of being eighty-five, he was only fifty-eight when he was found dead, under the influence of alcohol, in the Fort Ogden depot, July 14, 1921.

**Telling time: 15 minutes**
**Audience: 4th grade - adult**

*Bone Mizell has been described as a cowboy's cowboy. While there is no doubt he did many humorous things that were never recorded, he probably didn't do half the things that have been credited to him. However, he was a legend in his own time — a very popular character. Many people liked him when he was alive, and many people still enjoy hearing stories about his capricious life. A word of warning to the teller: do not yield to the temptation to tell one incident after another about Bone Mizell. Almost any Florida cowhunter can tell you a few, and fifteen or twenty minutes of his antics is all that most audiences will want to hear at one time.*

# Four Female Giants

**P**appy" **Smith lived in Racepond**, near Folkston, Georgia. He had seven daughters. Three of them were of ordinary size, married, and raised families. But four of his daughters were extremely large — more than six feet tall, strong as field hands, and proficient at jobs that were considered to be for men only. Although two of these female giants married, none of them had children.

The oldest was named Sarah. She was six feet four inches tall, and when she was sixteen, married a man named McLain. Shortly after the wedding, he was hanged for killing a man.

To earn a living, Widow Sarah Smith McLain ran a crosstie camp for a short time, then moved to Waycross, Georgia, and operated a barbershop. She advertised her craft by saying that she could "shave a man three days under the skin."

From Waycross, she headed south, and in 1905 arrived in Dade County, Florida. Evidently, she traveled the entire distance alone in an ox cart, with a shotgun resting against the seat. The cart was followed by two hounds as scrawny as the oxen which pulled it.

She camped where night caught her, but she had a way of making friends, and people never seemed to mind putting her up. She refused to sleep in a bed, preferring a pallet on the floor.

In Dade County, she worked on a farm, grubbing palmettos, hauling limestone rock, and plowing. Everyone started referring to her as the "Ox Woman." In Miami, she was a great curiosity. When she went by, people came out of their homes and places of business to see her. Her wardrobe consisted of a pair of men's work shoes, two dresses, and a black sunbonnet.

After working one season for the farmer, the Ox Woman set up camp and farmed on a key in what is now part of the Everglades National

Park. She also hunted deer and peddled the venison among the farmers and grove owners of South Dade.

Back in Racepond, two of her sisters, Nancy, who was called "Big Nancy," and Hannah, who was called "Big Six," were cutting crossties and chipping "catfaces" on pine trees. They were never married. But Lydia, who could not write her name, was making money. She contracted the cutting of crossties and operated a turpentine still. She also owned cattle and traded land.

In 1909, Sarah, the Ox Woman, called Sadie by her family, received a letter from them saying that her younger sister Hannah, or Big Six, had left home and was living in the town of Everglades. The family wanted Sadie to check on Hannah to make sure that she was all right.

The Ox Woman inquired about the place where Big Six lived, and found that it was "t'other side of Florida," seventy-five miles away, beyond the sawgrass-covered Everglades and Big Cypress Swamp. No highway crossed southern Florida at that time. She was told that to reach Big Six she would have to drive her oxen north to Melbourne, cross the state to Tampa, travel south to Fort Myers, and then take a boat — a total of three hundred slow miles.

We don't know the exact route the Ox Woman took, but with only her hounds and oxen, she crossed the Everglades.

In   1910, two years before the opening of the drainage canals, the Everglades were much like the ancient Indians had known them. Indian trails crossed the cypress strands long before the white man came, so the Ox Woman might have been able to follow old trails through the swamps north of Turner River. Although she could have had no accurate charts, she must have talked to those who knew the country.

There must have been times when the Ox Woman had to chop her way, but she was handy with the ax. Her knowledge of living off the land afforded her plenty to eat and water to drink. But how about panthers, bears, snakes, and alligators? The Ox Woman was well acquainted with all these critters and reptiles long before she came to Florida, for she was reared on the edge of the Okefenokee Swamp.

The Ox Woman found her sister Hannah, or Big Six. She was earning a living cutting buttonwood for the making of charcoal. She could cut more wood than any man. Ox Woman preferred to farm, and finding no land which was suitable for farming in the town of Everglades, Ox Woman decided to go to Immokalee, thirty-five miles north. Several miles east of Immokalee, along the edge of a cypress swamp, she found an Indian mound, about ten acres in size. Here, near a canoe landing used by pre-Columbian Indians, the big woman built herself a palmetto shack.

Shortly after her sister left, Big Six went to work for Ed Watson, who had a sugarcane farm and syrup factory at Chatham Bend in the Ten Thousand Islands, twenty miles south of Chokoloskee Island.

It seems that Ed Watson was hiring labor on the mainland, taking them to his place on the island, and when they became too insistent on their pay, he would do away with them and go hire more laborers. It is believed that "Bloody" Watson killed as many as fifty of his workers. Some of the bodies he buried, others he weighted and threw in a near-by river. When Big Six wanted to get her pay, Watson paid her in his usual manner, then slashed open her abdomen, tied sash weight to the body and dumped it into the bay — but that was his undoing. The body was so large that it came to the surface.

It was in the middle of October, 1910, when a clam fisherman and his young son were going up the Chatham River and the boy spotted a huge foot sticking out of the water. But the father was nearsighted and reprimanded his son for imagining things. When they returned later, the body to which the foot belonged had risen partly out of the water. The fisherman recognized the body as that of Hannah, or Big Six. The fisherman and his son spotted two other bodies. They hurried to Pavilion Key, a clam-fishing center, and spread the alarm.

A posse was formed. They found the bodies, then went looking for Watson. Watson was killed in the shoot-out that followed.

And what happened to the Ox Woman? About 1915, she pulled up stakes at her Indian mound farm near Immokalee and moved to a site near Fort Denaud, north of the Caloosahatchee River. In 1919, she died after suffering a stroke and was buried in the Fort Denaud Cemetery.

**Telling time: 12-13 minutes**
**Audience: 4th grade - adult**

*This story of four sisters is fascinating, and the story of Bloody Watson is gruesome, and each gives us a glimpse of the life and culture of its day. You might want to explain that buttonwood is a hard, slow-burning wood which is difficult to cut but excellent for cooking cane juice into syrup. "Catfaces" is jargon for the way pine trees are scored to gather pine rosin for making turpentine. This is an excellent story to use in connection with Florida geography.*

# How Orlando Got Its Name & Kept Its Courthouse

I t was full moon, in September of 1835, when a company of U.S. soldiers, reinforced by several cowboys, were trailing a band of hostile Indians through the Lake Jessup swamp. The setting sun gave warning of approaching night, and the captain commanded the company to make camp at Sandy Beach Lake (the old name of Lake Eola).

Quickly, camp was pitched and the horses fed. Soon the coffeepots were bubbling and frying pans sizzling. The hasty meal over, all the soldiers lay down to sleep. That is, all save one: a tall young man with dark hair named Orlando Reeves, who drew sentinel duty. He was trustworthy, eagle-eyed, and quick on the trigger, so the men felt secure with him on watch.

Faithfully, he paced back and forth in the bright moonlight. The hours dragged slowly by, and he was fighting drowsiness and fatigue. He stopped and rubbed his eyes. Strange, he thought, he had not noticed that log near those bushes. He continued on his patrol, and then retraced his steps. Now, there were more logs, and, even as he looked, they started rolling toward him.

"Indians!" He gave the alarm, knowing full well it meant his death. He fell, pierced by more than a dozen poisoned arrows.

For some time arrows whizzed and guns boomed, but somewhere near what is now Orange, Church, and Pine Streets the battle ended. The Indians fled, pursued by the soldiers.

Returning to camp, the soldiers found Orlando Reeves cold in death. They dug a grave beneath a tall pine, wrapped him in his blanket, and laid him to rest with a prayer.

The place became known as "Orlando's Grave." Travelers along the trail, pointing to the pine, would say: "Thar's Orlander's grave, and not fer from hit is a small spring. A right smart place fer campin'."

Five years before this battle, in 1830, the ninth county in Florida had been formed. It was named Mosquito County and included all of what is now Orange and Seminole, most of Lake, and part of Osceola, Sumter, and Volusia Counties. Because of the Indian Wars, the 1840 U.S. Census showed only seventy-three people living in Mosquito County.

In 1845 the name was changed to Orange County, and an election was held to determine where the county seat would be located. Enterprise, the incumbent, Apopka (then known as The Lodge), Fort Reid, and Fort Gatlin were all in the running. Fort Gatlin won, and the question of a name came up. The post office was known as Jernigan, and the little settlement was frequently spoken of as Fort Gatlin.

It was during a heated discussion that Judge Speer, a devotee of Shakespeare, arose, and said, "The place is often spoken of as Orlando's grave. Drop the last word, and let this new county seat be called Orlando." And so it was.

Then came the need of a courthouse. Out in the pine woods, near the old Church Street depot, stood an old deserted two-pen log house with dirt floors and no windows. In the east room, the first county officials opened their offices.

In October 1857, Benjamin F. Caldwell, for five dollars, deeded about four acres of land, to be the site of Orange County's courthouse, with the stipulation that it was to be known as the original town of Orlando.

The year 1870 marked a new era. The population of Orange County was now 2,195. While the wounds of the Civil War were not healed and, due to the lack of labor, cotton planting was a thing of the past, orange fever was rapidly rising.

It was in this year, 1870, that General Henry S. Sanford, former U.S. minister to Belgium, came to Florida and bought a large tract of land. He planted an orange grove a few miles out in the country, which he named Belair Grove. He next platted a town site to bear his name, which he vainly hoped would become the metropolis of Florida. It was located across Lake Monroe from Enterprise and a mile from old Mellonville. Here he built a large wharf, the Sanford Hotel, and grubbed out the streets. He presented to the Holy Cross Church a picture brought from Belgium, and then, he decided, the county seat must be moved from Orlando to his new town.

Simple enough, he thought; just call a meeting and settle the matter right then and there. He could already envision a fine new courthouse adorning his new town. Meetings were called, but it proved to be more difficult than anticipated. True, some were in favor of the move, but always there was the report of one Jacob Summerlin, the Cracker Cattle King, who was opposed and working against the move. So, after many futile attempts to get this cow hunter to come to him, General Sanford decided to make the long tiresome trip from Sanford to Orlando to confront his opposition.

On his arrival in Orlando, he went to the only hotel the town then had. High brow and high hat, he walked up the steps. There was no bell, and his repeated knocks failed to bring the landlord to the door. Out of patience, and out of sorts, he sat down in one of the rocking chairs on the porch. It was while there that he spotted a man, apparently asleep, on the floor at the south end of the porch. There was a wide-brimmed hat over his face, and he had on cowboy boots. His shirt was open at the neck, and he was using saddlebags for a pillow.

Ah, Sanford thought, this may be a lucky thing after all. This fellow, no doubt, knows the troublemaker and can give me some insight on the best means of bringing him to terms.

The general crossed the floor, cleared his throat, and with a pompous wave of his hand, said condescendingly, "You look like a native."

"Then I look as I oughter," answered the cow hunter.

"Perhaps you have met this self-styled cattle king, Jacob Summerlin?"

"Wal, no, I've never met him, but my wife knows him purty well. She met him some time ago, before we moved to Orlando; so I've heard considerable about his doin's."

"Then tell me, if you can, why this ignorant cattle man dares to defy me, General Henry S. Sanford, late U.S. minister to Belgium, in my efforts to move the courthouse to the new town, where it properly ought to be?"

"Wal, I reckon he thinks Orlando is a purty good place, and people are jest sorter used to tending to court and doing their trading here."

"I care nothing for what he thinks! He will learn that his stubborn opposition and insolent refusal to agree with me will gain him nothing. For I say the county seat is going to be moved to Sanford."

The cow hunter sat up. "You may be General Sanford and think you're agoin' to move the courthouse, but I'm Jake Summerlin, and I say, there on Main Street stands the Orange County courthouse, and there it will stand when you and I, our children and grandchildren have long since passed away." He then lay back down and resumed his quiet meditation.

The next morning, the commissioners met in the old courthouse. On one side of the room sat Jacob Summerlin, a native, who knew the old pioneers. He knew the simplicity of their lives, their honesty and integrity, their poverty and courage.

On the other side sat General Sanford, a Yankee, who was unaccustomed to physical labor and crude living conditions. He was egotistical and ambitious, with a mental picture of a wonderful city bearing his name.

When new business was called for, the general arose and, in glowing terms, described the benefit to the whole county from the change.

Jacob Summerlin sat quietly. When General Sanford sat down he stood and asked if the general had finished his speech.

"I have," came the curt reply.

"Then I will make my offer," said Jacob Summerlin. "The county seat has been located here by the free will of the majority of the settlers, and the land has been deeded for that purpose. I stand here ready to build a ten-thousand-dollar courthouse and if the county is ever able to pay me back, that will be good. If not, that will be all right with me."

The offer was quickly accepted, and the county seat remained in Orlando.

**Telling time: 18–20 minutes**
**Audience: 4th grade – adult**

*We enjoy hearing about places where we have been. This story has widespread appeal because people from the four corners of the world come to Orlando today, and many are familiar with Lake Eola and the courthouse. They may not know that it was not until 1913 that Seminole County was formed and Sanford chosen as its county seat. Orange County has had several new courthouses since the one that Jacob Summerlin financed, but all of them have remained in Orlando on Main Street. (The name of Main Street was changed to Magnolia in the mid-nineteen hundreds.)*

# Jake, King of the Crackers

**J**acob Summerlin, known as "Jake, King of the Crackers" was the first white child born in Florida after Spain ceded the territory to the United States. He was born February 22, 1821, near Lake City, then known as Alligator.

When he was seven years old, he could ride a horse and crack a whip. When he was sixteen, the second Indian war broke out, and all the friendly Indians became warriors.

Jake's father knew that he must move his family to a safer shelter than that of their isolated home, so they packed the wagons and set out for a settlement called Newnansville. Other families came pouring in from every quarter, and soon between one and two thousand people were gathered where only a few families had been living.

The men and older boys labored day and night digging a trench and building a double wall of logs (a log behind each crack between the logs in front) fifteen feet high. The hard work made for healthy appetites, and soon, food became scarce.

Jake's father decided he must go back to his home to get food. He asked Jake and his brother to saddle their horses and come along, so they, too, could bring back food.

Because of the father's involvement in the war with the Creeks in Georgia, he was a prime target. The Seminoles vowed they would kill him and burn his home.

It was after dark when the Summerlins got to their home, but they found the house still standing and the food untouched — a bank of sweet potatoes in the yard, plenty of meat in the smoke-house, and corn in the barn. They packed up as much as they dared to put on their horses, knowing they might have to ride for their lives going back to the fortification.

When the horses were loaded, they tied them close to the house, and the boys lay down on the floor to sleep. But the father stood watch. As he watched and listened, he gave thought as to why his place was still untouched.

As he might have guessed, the Indians had not forgotten their threat. They were just waiting, hoping that he would return. Even now, the enemy had been alerted to his and his sons' presence and were creeping up on them, intending to kill him and his boys and burn his home at one time.

As the father listened with keen ears, a sound broke the stillness of the midnight — a sheep bell! The sheep were rushing toward the sheep pen. He knew, by the way they ran, that they had been startled by the approach of men.

"Up boys and out! The Indians are here!" he cried.

In a minute, each was in his saddle and riding for his life. A few minutes later, the glow of the burning buildings lit the sky.

It was their ability to find their way through the woods in the dark that enabled them to make it back to the fortification.

The Indians did not take kindly to being betrayed by the sheep. They penned up more than one hundred of the bleating creatures, and one by one skinned them alive!

During the hot summer that followed, there were sickness and death behind the log walls of the hastily made fort. The Indians seemed to have deserted this part of Florida, and a careless sense of security started to pervade. Mothers started taking their children outside the walls. Old men and boys, who were now the sole defenders of the place, went to hunt wild turkey and other game. In the shade of trees, they cooked and ate during the day and only returned to the fort at night.

Carpenter Horn, a man who could not be idle, made wheels and cleaned and mounted a small, old cannon, which, along with a bushel of six-pound balls, had been discarded and left behind by troops traveling south.

One day, old man Pendarvis went out to see if he could kill a deer. As he followed a narrow stream where deer often came to drink, his old deer-hound stopped suddenly with a peculiar low growl. Pendarvis crept forward until he saw two Indians, armed and painted with war paint, creeping up the brook.

He ran back to give the alarm, and a wild scene followed — women shrieking and rushing to the fort, carrying sometimes their own babies and sometimes others picked up by mistake. Men were bewildered and panic-stricken. There were only three hundred old men and boys, and there were the lives of a thousand women and children at stake.

Carpenter Horn wheeled the cannon into place, and when the Indians made their first dash at the fort, he fired the cannon at them, and killed two. This came as a surprise to the attacking party. They were acquainted with guns, but they had never heard of a cannon. The power and the noise of the weapon so overwhelmed them that some of them fled, but others charged again. There was a fierce battle, but Carpenter Horn with his cannon finally won. Had it not been for the deer-hound, the forewarning of old man Pendarvis, and the cannon, no doubt all of the inhabitants of the place would have been killed, as it was Osceola and five hundred of his braves slipping up that brook.

What part young Jake Summerlin had in this battle is not clear, but we do know that he lived to prosper in the cattle business.

Even as a young man he could wield, with accuracy, a cow whip eighteen feet long, with only an eighteen-inch handle, often referred to as a drag. He received some calves as a gift from his father. He cared for them well and eventually became the owner of large herds. He shipped thousands of cattle to Cuba each year, making a great profit on every shipload.

He bought land, built wharves, and came to own houses, lakes, and citrus groves. He owned the wharf at Punta Rassa (the chief shipping point for cattle sold in Key West and Cuba) and one thousand acres of land adjacent to it. Stories of his riches spread, and he came to be called the "King of the Crackers." The title or nickname amused and pleased him, for he was proud of his Cracker heritage and appreciated the lessons learned from his early hardships and dangers. He continued to dress, live, talk, and trade as a poor man might, but he gave to the poor and defended the cause of the fatherless against the land sharks as only a rich man can.

Spaniards regarded him with awe — a man who was indifferent to wealth but couldn't be cheated, who wouldn't gamble, and who never smoked or drank. Indians respected him as a man who kept his word.

Jacob Summerlin, the famous pioneer cattle king, died in Orlando, November 1, 1893. He was one of the most picturesque figures in Florida's history. Without a formal education, he amassed a great fortune. He was entirely unpretentious, but very generous in support of worthy public causes — especially the education of the youth of the state.

An impressive incident in his civic contributions was his financing of Orange County's fourth courthouse, thus thwarting pompous General Sanford's efforts to move the county seat to his town. He gave Lake Eola and forty to sixty feet surrounding it to Orlando for a park. He also gave the site and erected imposing buildings in Bartow for an institution of higher education. This institution, which in the mid-twentieth century was replaced by the Bartow High School, bore his name, and Summerlin Avenue in Orlando is named in his honor — small tokens of appreciation for one who did so much. But the many lives that he touched with his helping hand must have been the reward most appreciated by Jake, the King of the Crackers.

**Telling time: 15 minutes**
**Audience: 4th grade – adult**

*Jake Summerlin was a man of small stature — soft-spoken and gentle — but could get very tough when the need arose. He had a good sense of humor and a quick wit. He was a very wealthy man with very simple taste. Some of his descendants do not believe that a portrait showing a man with a corncob pipe in his mouth is of him, because it was a well-known fact that he did not smoke. But a close scrutiny of the features shows a close resemblance to those of the man in a more formal portrait. Knowing his personality, it is not hard to imagine that a reporter traveled to Florida for the express purpose of interviewing this man, dressed him in the costume in which he is shown, and took his picture as "King of the Crackers." Jacob Summerlin's life and character are worthy of study.*

# Seminole Invasion of Key West

T he U.S. government set the first day of 1836 as the date for all Indians to be out of the state of Florida. As the date to leave neared, the Indians came together — not to leave their Florida homes, but to fight for them. The Seminoles were on a rampage.

A few months before, Major Francis Dade and his command were recalled from Key West to Fort Brooke (now Tampa) where they were reinforced with additional troops. On December 28th while enroute to Fort King (now Ocala), he and 110 United States regulars were ambushed near Bushnell. All were killed or wounded and left for dead, but at least two (possibly three) privates lived to give an eyewitness account of the tragedy.

The news of the massacre shocked every heart, and there seemed to be a general feeling that Key West would be the next point of attack. Why? It is hard to say, unless it was because the island was so defenseless. The naval force had been withdrawn, and now the army barracks stood deserted on the beach a mile from the town.

The men in town organized themselves into a guard. They were well armed and kept a patrolled watch night and day. Yet every night the islanders went to bed with the feeling that, before morning, they might be awakened by Seminole war whoops.

For several weeks all went well, but one night it came — the signal that the Indians were coming. It was about two o'clock in the morning when the patrol came tapping on windows saying, "Get up! Get up at once! They've come! The signal drum is beating at the barracks!"

Everyone was up immediately. Coming from the direction of the barracks was certainly the sound of a muffled drum.

The men were soon armed and ready. As quickly and as silently as possible, they planned their strategy. A reconnaissance seemed unnecessary, for without a doubt, the enemy was there. They felt sure, within a mile of them, there was such a force of Indians that they would all be scalped before sunup. But to be absolutely sure would be better than to labor under suspense; so, at last, a party of the bravest and most able-bodied men volunteered to form the front line of defense.

As silently as ghosts, these men stole through the gloriously bright, tropical moonlight. Their sweat stank of fear, for they knew that the infernal war whoop might come from behind any bush or tree.

As they neared the barracks and the sound of that muffled drum grew louder, they began to feel the scalping knives and see the war paint and feathers.

In the edge of the low woods, approaching the clearing in front of the barracks, they stopped, afraid that even their breath might betray them. Then they struggled to go through the thicket without a sound. When they reached the clearing, everything was as still as the death they feared. Nothing could be heard but the low wash of the waves on the beach nearby — and the tap, tap, tap of the drum. There was nothing to be seen either — nothing but the old barracks with its broad, open porch.

When the suspense seemed more than they could bear, one man cautiously stepped out into the clearing. Then he took another step; then a few steps further. Then, with a loud shriek of nervous laughter, he jerked his hand from his gun and pointed to the enemy.

Feeling sure that he had cracked under the pressure, his comrades sprang to his side. From there, they beheld the feared Seminole invasion. Hundreds of braves in gaudy war paint and fully armed? No. It was only one old, mangy dog seated on the top of an empty cistern, hitting it with his wagging tail.

**Telling time: 7-8 minutes**
**Audience: 3rd grade - adult**

*This story is taken from the eyewitness account of H. P. Huse which appeared in the* Wide-Awake *magazine, published shortly after the Seminole Wars of 1835-42. It serves to remind us that certain atmospheric conditions play havoc with sound waves, and that fears overwork our imaginations. The teller needs to steadily build the suspense in this story right from the beginning. In order to do this you must build on the fear which is always present during a war: Both sides play for keeps and build support and sympathy by painting the enemy as being bloodthirsty and cruel.*

# Introduction

# Tall Tales & Nonsense Stories

**W** **hile tall tales and nonsense stories** are always crowd-pleasers, all tall tales or nonsense stories will not please every audience.

Young children enjoy nonsense and repetitious stories if the story is about something with which they can identify. Tall tales of fishing, hunting, and sports are probably a sure bet for a male audience, and the female audience will likely enjoy tall tales about dieting, romance, and fashion.

The success of a tall tale or nonsense story, like other humor, depends greatly on the mood of the audience and the ability of the teller. Timing, enunciation, and voice projection is vital.

"Epaminondas," a Southern nonsense story, has been told to receptive audiences for decades, and "Moonshine Hollow" is superb for a mixed audience. Although, "Epaminondas" is much better told than read, it can be successfully read aloud, but telling is essential for the success of "Moonshine Hollow."

Do Tell!

# Epaminondas

paminondas might be classified as a slow learner, but you can't blame him for that. And you will have to give him credit for always doing just what his mammy told him to do.

Now, Epaminondas liked to go to see his auntie, who lived about a mile down the sand road from his house. She had more of this world's goods than Epaminondas and his mammy. And Auntie was always ready to share.

One day when Epaminondas went to see his auntie, she had made a cake. Now, it wasn't just an ordinary cake — no. It was twelve layers high, with all this chocolate goo between the layers, and on the top, and on the sides. She gave Epaminondas a nice slice, and he was sure it was the best cake in the world.

When he was ready to go home, his auntie gave Epaminondas a big piece of that cake to take home for him and his mammy.

Epaminondas was proud to be the bearer of such a great gift. He took that cake in his hand, and started along home. The further he walked, the tighter he closed his hand; so, by the time he got home, all he had in his hand was a little dough-ball and some chocolate goo between his fingers.

"What's that you got, son?" asked his mammy.

"The best cake you've ever et!" answered Epaminondas. "Auntie sent it to ya."

His mammy's mouth started watering. She looked at his hand, and said, "Epaminondas, you ain't got the sense you wus born with. Son, when someone gives ya a piece of cake, put it on top of yer haid, put yer hat over it and walk along home. Ya think ya can 'member that?"

"Yessum, Mammy."

The next time that Epaminondas went to see his auntie, she was churning butter. And she gave him some of that sweet cream, homemade butter on hot biscuits with plenty of guava jelly. He had to admit that it was as good as that chocolate cake. When he was ready to go home, Auntie gave him a nice big cake of that butter to take home with him.

Epaminondas started home. "Mammy is gonna be so proud of this here butter," he said to himself. "I gotta take it home jest lack she told me to, and she'll be proud of me."

So he put it on his head, put his hat over it, and started home. But it was a hot day, and soon that butter was running all down in his eyes, all down in his ears, and all down his back. When he got home all the butter he had was on him.

His mammy took one look at him, and said, "Laud have mercy, Epaminondas, what have ya got all over ya?"

"Butter, Mammy. Auntie sent it to ya."

"Oh, me, Epaminondas, ya ain't got the sense ya wus born with. Don't ya know that when someone gives ya butter, yore suppose ter go to the garden, and git ya a big cabbage leaf. Put the butter on the cabbage leaf, and then take it to the spring, and cool it, and cool it, and cool it, until ya really get it cool. Then ya can bring it along home. Do ya understand?

"Yes, Mammy."

"Do you think that you can 'member that?"

"Yes, Mammy."

The next time that Epaminondas went to see his auntie, her dog had had puppies. And his auntie gave Epaminondas the pick of the litter. He was so proud of that puppy, and he knew just how he had to take it home. He went into the garden, and got two of the biggest cabbage leaves he could find. Then he took the puppy to the spring, and cooled it, and cooled it, and cooled it, until he got it really cool. Then he took it along home.

His mammy took one look, and threw up her hands. "Laud, have mercy, Epaminondas, what have ya got?"

"A puppy, Mammy. Auntie gave it to me."

"Epaminondas, ya ain't got the sense ya wus born with. Look what you've gone and done. You've almost drown dis pore little puppy. Don't ya know, when somebody gives ya a puppy, you must reach way down deep in ya pocket, and git a ball of string. Take one end of the string, and tie it round the puppy's neck, and then ya can jest lead him along home. Do ya understand that?"

"Yessum, Mammy."

The next time that Epaminondas went to see his auntie, she was making bread. Oh, the smell of that homemade bread — fresh out of the

sand-acre field and roped it off with barbed wire charged with electricity. Although Gator Tadd would not let a living soul inside, people knew that was where he launched his sky hooks to hold his scaffold for his sky painting. You could hear some big booming sounds, like big fireworks, and folks figured that he was firing his sky hooks out of a cannon, and that they fastened onto the sound barrier.

After a while, if you took a spyglass, you could see Gator Tadd's long scaffold raising up, up, up in the air and Gator Tadd, looking about as big as a spider, squatting on it.

But that too played out. It wasn't that people didn't like his sky painting any more, but the airplanes got to buzzing around as thick as flies around a molasses barrel, and one day, one of the pesky things brushed against his scaffold and upset Gator Tadd's paints. After that, Gator Tadd was never seen in Orlando again. The pilot of the plane said that trying to catch his paint, Gator Tadd lost his balance and fell. Some figure that the big bull gators, which were having a convention in the swamp at the time, put a bridle on him before he caught his breath after the fall.

But that day he was working on a big job in blue, yellow, and green. Of course, you know that blue and yellow makes green when it's mixed, and that paint got mixed! Many people declare that Gator Tadd land d in the middle of one of those deep lakes in the swamp, and by the tim· he swam to shore, an advertising agent was there with a contract in hand to sign him up as the "Green Giant."

Now, you'll have to decide for yourself what happened to Gator Tadd, because I want to have no part in influencing a conclusion which would have to be made from hearsay. But you can look on any Florida state map and verify that they *still* call not only his thousand-acre field, but all that 576,000 acres, The Green Swamp.

**Telling time: 18-19 minutes**
**Audience: 4th grade - adult**

*This is an excellent example of a tall tale. The teller puts no emphasis on the exaggerations — just throws them in the text and acts as if he expects everyone to believe them, and they will — for a short time. Don't expect to have too much laughter unless you have in your audience some sharp 4th and 5th graders who want you to know that you are not pulling the wool over their eyes. But the lack of laughter does not spell doom. The audience will enjoy the story if it is told well.*

# Moonshine Hollow

**S**al Itchigum here, a lookin' fer my feller. Anybody seed Bill? Bill who? I might've known a bunch of ole whippersnappers wouldn't know who Bill wus.

Well, Bill ain't his real name. I jest call him that. His real name is Bilious — Bilious Buttonbuster. And he's my feller. Leastwise, he wus.

T'other day I was ironin' over a hot fire when I heard someone a comin'. I knowed it wus Bill so I ran real quick and got me a pan of water and rinched off my face, smoothed down my hair, pinched my cheeks, and rubbed my lips so they'd be nice and rosy. Then I got out my store-bought co-log-ne. You know what store-bought co-log-ne is, don't you? That channel number five? And I put a little dab under each arm, and back of each year. Then, I went to the door to meet my feller. Well, it weren't Bill, at all. Some pan-handler from up the State summers.

Well, I'd already got all gussied up, and I wasn't wantin' to waste my store-bought co-log-ne; so I said, "You might as well pull ya up a cheer and sit a spell."

He looked up at the sky, and said, "Looks lak there's a cloud acomin' up so I b'lieve I will."

He hunkered back in that cheer, and started pullin' out all this here stuff he had to sell. He pretty soon had it scattered ever which away all over my porch so I knowed he wasn't goin' no place. That suited me alright 'cause I wus glad to sit a spell in that swang, and I started tellin' him 'bout my feller, Bill.

After a while, he said, "You know, I just might have seed yore feller, the other day."

I said, "What do ya mean — you might have seed him?"

"Well," he said, "I seed two fellers out here at Astatula t'other day, and one of 'em might have been yore feller."

"What makes you think so? Did he look like my feller?"

"Like I say, there wus two of 'em. One looked like Sandy Clause,'cept he had on bib-overalls and a blue denim shirt, but the other feller had his hair slicked back 'till his head looked like a melon with a big nose and two floppy ears."

I didn't like that description of my feller, and I told him so. I axed him if he didn't say who he wus, or somethin'?

He said, "Oh, he said somethin'. He said plenty, but I can't truthfully say he ever did say who he wus."

"Well, what did he say?" I asked.

And that ole peddler said, "Well, now, let me see iffen I can tell you jest what that feller said. He said, 'Me and my pa, here, lives out here about a mile, a mile and a half, or two miles. T'other day pa says to me, ter lets go larpin', tarpin', coon-skin huntin' if I keered? I axed him, I didn't keer; so, we called all the dogs together 'cept ole Shorty, and then we called 'im too. We went down the hill till we got to the top of the mountain, and we treed one. It wus in a tall, slick, sycamore saplin' — 'bout ten feet above the top, out on an ole chestnut snag. Told pa I'd better shake 'im out if he didn't keer. And he axed me, he didn't keer. So, I clumbed up, and shook, and shook, till I heard somethin' fall. Turned 'round, and saw, it wus me, and all the dogs wus on top of me, but ole Shorty, and he wus on top of me, too. Told Pa ter knock 'im off, iffen he keered and he axed me he didn't keer; so, he picked up a pine-knot, and knocked 'em all off but ole Shorty, and then he knocked 'im off too.

"'We went saunderin' on down the creek, and pretty soon, we treed another one. This one wus in a huckleberry log — 'bout two feet through at the little end. Told Pa, I'd better cut 'im out, to save time, if he keered, and he axed me he didn't keer; so, I picked up the ax, and the very first lick I made, I cut ole Shorty's long, smooth tail off, right close up behind his ears — like to ruin my dog; so, I told Pa, that wus 'nough huntin' fer one day, and we started fer the house. On the way home, we saw all the pumpkins in the pig-patch. Told Pa, we'd better chase 'em out, if he keered, and he axed me he didn't keer. We chased 'em pumpkins all over that pig-patch till I kinda got mad at one, and picked 'im up by the tail, and slammed his brains out 'gainst a pig. Pa got real mad 'bout that, and talked to me lak I wus a red-headed step-child, he did. But we got 'em out, fixed up the gate, and shut the fence, and started fer the house.

"'Then Pa told me to shuck and shell 'em a bucket of slop, if I keered, and I axed him, I didn't keer. So I shucked and shelled 'em a bucket of slop.

"'Then I decided I'd go down to see my gal, Sal. Now, Sal lives in Moonshine Holler on Tough Street — the further you go, the tougher it gits, and Sal lives in the very last house. It's a big white house, painted green, with two front doors, on the back. You can't miss her place 'cause it's got a mortgage on it, and runnin' water in every room in the house — when it rains.

"'Bein', it wus Sunday, I told Pa, I'd ride if he keered, and he axed me, he didn't keer; so I went out, put the bridle on the lot, the horse on the saddle, led the fence up by the gate and the horse got on. We went saunterin' off down the road, kinda gently lak at first, till a stump, over in one corner of the horse, got scared at the fence and raired-up, and throwed me, face-foremost, flat of my back in the middle of the road, slap-dab in the middle of a ditch 'bout ten feet deep, right in the middle of a briar patch. Tore one of the sleeves outten my Sunday-go-to-meetin' pants, but I got up, peered to me lak I wasn't hurt, brushed the horse off the dirt, got back on, and went leadin' 'im on down the road.

"'When I got to Sal's house, I knowed she wus glad ter see me, 'cause she had both doors shut wide open, and the winders nailed down.

"'I got off, hitched the fence to the horse, went in, threw my hat in the fireplace, spit on the bed, and down I sot in a big armchair — on a stool.

"'Now, me and Sal talked 'bout craps, and politics, and all other kind of ticks. Then, Sal 'lows, "Bill, let's go down to the peach orchard and get some pears to make a huckleberry pie fer dinner."

"'I axed her, I didn't keer.

"'We started down to the orchard, and I wus walkin' jest as close to my gal as I could — her on one side of the road and me on the t'other.

"'When I got to the peach orchard, I told Sal, I'd climb up the pear tree and shake down some apples, if she keered, and she axed me, she didn't keer; so, I clumbed up, and shook and shook till the limb I wus standin' on broke and threw me right ter straddle of a barbed-wire fence, with both feet on the same side — skinned my right shin, jest above my left elbow, and I told Sal right then and thar, that that'd be the last time I'd be in Moonshine Holler, and I ain't been back since. I ain't.'"

Well, when I heard that pan-handler say my feller wasn't comin' back no more, I got so upset, I couldn't sleep, I couldn't eat. Why, I wasted away to nearly nothin' 'fore I 'cided that if I could find 'im — if I could eye-ball 'im — I might get 'im to change his mind.

But you know, I've 'cided that I've lost 'nough sleep, missed 'nough meals, and spent 'nough time, lookin' fer that man. I'm jest standin' here to tell all you ladies — give you fair warnin' — if you've got a feller, and ya think anything atall of 'im, you'd better hog-tie 'im 'cause I'm out to git myself another feller.

**Telling time: 14–15 minutes**
**Audience: high school – adult**

*Although this story has long been the favorite of my two daughters and my niece, and I have had a few women become almost hysterical laughing at my telling of "Moonshine Holler," I think of it as a man's story. Men do enjoy it. It requires time to learn: you need to know it so well that you say the backward expressions automatically. There is a rhythm to it that needs to be maintained for the best results.*

# Introduction

# Gator Tales

**I**n the gator tale category are to be found the storylines of folk
and fairy tales that have been brought here by the many cultures
which make up the polyglot society of Florida. While the storyline
is often old, the atmosphere is fresh and light. Gator tales reflect the
flora, fauna, and topography of Florida, but do not necessarily involve
alligators.

Do Tell!

# Ole One Eye

There was this here ole woman, lived out here in Franklin County. She worked so hard, and saved so good, that she wus purtin' nigh rich. She squirreled away all her gold in an ole sock, and hid it in the chimney corner.

She worked all day a plantin' and takin' care of her cotton patch, and raisin' her food, and every night she'd sit there in her little cabin, a rockin' and cardin' her cotton or wool — scritch, scratch, scritch, scratch. This way she could spin it into thread during the heat of the day, when she couldn't work outside.

Now, this ole woman didn't only work hard, she saved good. She wouldn't spend her money fer nothin' she didn't have to have.

She didn't have a watch nor a clock, but she was not about to spend her money fer one. And, to tell you the truth, she really didn't need one. She could tell the time of day, give or take a few minutes, by the shadows on the cracks in her porch floor. And at night? Well, she had figured out a way to tell time then, too.

She'd sit there a rockin' back and forth, a cardin' her fiber — scritch, scratch, scritch, scratch — and after a while she'd yawn. When she yawned three times, she figured it was bedtime so she'd get up, go to bed, and sleep till the roosters woke her up. This worked fine for her.

But the one thing she would spend her money for was dried mullet. She loved dried mullet. Every time she went to the crossroad store to sell her eggs, she'd get some dried mullet. One day, when she took her eggs to the store, she found that the dried mullet had gone up five cents on the pound.

"No-o-o! Not spendin' my money that a way! My ole hens ain't a layin' lak they oughter, and I ain't spendin' my money foolish-lak at all," she said, and she started to leave.

The storekeeper didn't want to miss a sale so he said, "Just a minute. I've got a big ole mullet here. Don't know what happened to it, but somehow it got one of its eyes knocked out. Iffen you want it, I'll let you have it fer three cents less on the pound."

Well, she couldn't turn down a bargain like that! She didn't care whether or not it had two eyes. She took that ole fish and started along home. As she walked along, she'd look at it, and smack her lips, and say, "Ole One-Eye." When she got home, she would have liked to just set down and et it all up, but she didn't know when she'd get another bargain so she decided she'd better make "Ole One-Eye" last awhile. She tied a string around its tail and hung it on a nail — just above where she kept her gold hid. Then day after day, she worked a raisin' her food, and night after night she sat there — rockin', back and forth, a cardin' her fiber — scritch, scratch, scritch, scratch. And when she had yawned three times, she'd get up, get her knife, cut a hunk off that fish, and eat it before goin' to bed. That way, she had something to look forward to all day, and that fish was goin' to last a long time.

Now about this time there were three robbers runnin' from the law, and they hid out on the edge of Tate's Hell Swamp. The leader of the gang was as mean as a Texas rattlesnake. He'd got into a fight and got one of his eyes knocked out so he was called Ole One-Eye. This gang got to goin' up to the crossroad store to get food, and they heard people talking about that old woman — how rich she wus.

And Ole One-Eye said, "Boys, we're goin' out there to that ole woman's place and get that gold."

And one night, that was what they decided they'd do. They went out there and hid in a cypress-head to case the place, but they couldn't see a thing.

So Ole One-Eye said to one of the other robbers, "You, you go over there and spy on that ole woman. When she goes to bed, come back and let us know so we can go and take her gold."

That robber didn't want to go over there by himself, but he was more afraid of Ole One-Eye than he was of that old woman. He went to the cabin and walked all around it, but he couldn't see anything because the doors were shut and the winders all shuttered-up. But after a while, in the chimney corner, he found a little chink where the mud had fallen out from between the logs — just under where she had that old one-eyed fish hanging. He stooped down and looked in. He could see her sitting there carding her fiber — scritch, scratch, scritch, scratch.

And just then she yawned once, looked over at that old one-eyed fish, and said, "There's the first one. When two more come, I'll get my knife and start cuttin'" and she smacked her lips.

The robber was sure she was looking straight at him. He jumped up and took off running back to that cypress-head. "Come on, let's get out of here. That old woman is a witch. She looked straight through the wall and said, 'That's one that's come, and when two more come, I'm getting my knife and start cuttin'.'"

"That's nothin' but a pop-eyed lie. You know, you jest got scared, that's all. You," — Ole One-Eye motioned to the other robber — "you go down there and spy on that old woman, and when she goes to bed, come back here and let us know so we can get her gold."

The other robber went over and started walking around the cabin. After a bit, he spotted the same chink. He looked in. She was still cardin' — scritch, scratch, scritch, scratch — and she yawned.

"Well, there's the second one. When one more comes, I can get my knife, and start cuttin'."

That robber jumped up and just hit a few of the high spots as he raced back to that cypress-head.

"Let's go from here. She is a witch, for sure. She looked right through that wall, and said that I was the second one, and when one more came she was gettin' her knife, and start cuttin'. We'd better make tracks!"

"Ya know," said Old One-Eye. "Sometimes, I'm ashamed to be associated with sech yeller-bellied cowards. Reckon I'll have to go over there and spy on that old woman myself. But y'all jest remember who did all the work when it's time to divide up the gold."

And with that he walked over to the cabin and started casing the place. He found the same chink. He put his one good eye up there where he could see.

She hadn't gone to bed. She was still rockin' back and forth, cardin' her fiber — scritch, scratch, scritch, scratch. Then she yawned. She put down her cards, looked over at the fish, and said, "Now, I'm gettin' my butcherin' knife and cut a big hunk outten Ole One-Eye."

You would have thought that robber had been shot out of a cannon. Back to that cypress-head he went. "Come on, men, let's get out of here, now! That old witch not only looked through the wall and saw me, she called me by name."

Those robbers ran into Tate's Hell Swamp and were never heard tell of in Franklin County again. And that old woman? Well, she is still working all day, and every night she sits there in her swamp-cabin cardin' her fiber. How? Scritch, scratch! Scritch, scratch!

**Telling time: 14–15 minutes**
**Audience: 3rd grade – adult**

*This is one of the most generic of stories. It is in the genre of gator tales because of its setting in Florida. It could be set anyplace with good results. Tate's Hell Swamp and how it got its name is an interesting study.*

*Legend has it that a man named Tate got lost then bitten by a rattlesnake in this big swamp in the Panhandle's Franklin County. He lived for over a week, crawling through the swamp still marked on maps as "Tate's Hell Swamp."*

*"Ole One Eye" is a crowd pleaser, and many times the audience will join in without your prompting as you demonstrate how the old woman carded her cotton and wool. Invite them to join in at the end if they don't. They will enjoy this bit of audience participation.*

# Ignorance Is Bliss

"**M**iriam, it is a lot of work**, but I'm glad we decided to sell the furniture ourselves rather than letting a dealer have it." Glenda wiped her brow and pushed her glasses up on her nose.

"I think it is kinda fun — a challenge. And if we play our cards right, we should be able to get premium prices for most of this old stuff. With today's clamor for antiques, as soon as it is known we are moving into smaller quarters, we'll be swamped with bargain hunters."

"Help me turn this desk over so I can burn the initials 'N W' on the bottom."

"That's right. It did belong to Noah Webster, didn't it?" Glenda chuckled as she crawled from the back of a headboard she was dating with a nail.

"Remember, all the bent-wood furniture in the sun parlor was made by Michael Thonet, himself," Miriam reminded her sister, and then asked, "What did we decide about the secretary?"

"I think we should apologize for the corner of the drop-door being chewed-up — explain that during the Civil War a Yankee soldier pried it open with his bayonet, looking for the family jewels." Glenda used an elongated Southern drawl, and both ladies giggled.

"With our deed to this place dating back to the Spanish occupation, everyone expects us to have a house full of antiques, so we shan't disappoint them," concluded Miriam.

"For several years, I've bemoaned the fact that we disposed of the old family furniture, but really, making antiques is proving to be more fun than just owning them."

"But we must remember to be subtle. If this sale gets noised about too much, dealers and experts will be coming out of the woodwork, and if they discover the fraud, they might try to disgrace our name."

"Don't say 'fraud'," implored Glenda. "Why, that sounds downright dishonest. We're only making happy mementos. The people who buy this old furniture can't afford many treasures, and it'll bring them hours of happiness thinking they have a real museum piece."

"Especially when they think they have discovered proof which we didn't know existed. So be sure they see it, but act completely ignorant of its existence."

"Sister, which of these two looks older?"

"Mmmm, both look as old as the pyramids."

"Don't need them to look that old," mused Miriam, admiring her success in aging the paper. She read the faded ink on one of the labels.

*20 August 1773*
*100 pounds Fyne green Tea*
*East India Company*
*London, England*

"Maybe you should tear or burn the edge so the day and actual weight are not legible. That might be information too easily disproved," suggested Glenda.

"This has to be our master stroke — converting Papa's old kindling box into a tea chest," Miriam said. "Let's put the old picnic paraphernalia back in here. It will keep the label from being too conspicuous."

"What unsuspecting buyer shall we try first?" asked Glenda.

"Let's pack up all our autographed first editions and then give the rest of our books to the college library. That will get us a tax deduction and a prospective buyer."

"That's right. Mr. Zimmerman is interested in antiques. Do you think he'll be smart enough to detect our little additions?"

"Not if we play it smart. And I figure, if we give the library the books, he'll feel obligated to buy something," Miriam said.

"Sister, you really have a good head for business."


Soon after lunch, Mr. Zimmerman arrived and examined the books that the Haynes sisters were offering to the college library.

"I have chosen twenty-six books which I believe the library will be able to use. The remainder, due to condition and/or content, will not be acceptable. An official letter of acknowledgment and appreciation will be mailed to you in the near future. For the present, here is a signed receipt for them and my sincere thanks." Mr. Zimmerman stacked the books into tote boxes and looked around the room. "Are you planning to sell any of your furnishings?"

"Yes. It breaks our hearts to part with our old family heirlooms, but we just won't have room for much in the apartment," Glenda said, wiping her eyes with the corner of her apron.

Miriam spoke up. "While we realize that family pieces have mostly sentimental value, we understand that the intrinsic value has increased some of late."

"Yes. The demand for both collectibles and genuine antiques has increased," Mr. Zimmerman said.

"We don't know anything about antiques or buying and selling. Maybe you could tell us what this old tea chest is worth," suggested Miriam.

"It has been in our family for generations. As long as I can remember, we have kept our picnic ware stored in it," added Glenda.

"Is that why you call it a tea chest?" Mr Zimmerman asked, looking at the large, footed box.

"Oh, no. It is our understanding that England shipped loose tea to the colonies in this very chest. It was footed to protect the tea from dampness in the ship's hole. Of course, we have no way to verify that."

"Did you have a price in mind?" Mr. Zimmerman asked, trying to get an idea of the Haynes sisters' dollar value.

"Well, we know it is a little rough so we were thinking maybe in the neighborhood of three hundred dollars."

Mr. Zimmerman raised the lid. The corners were not dovetailed, and the nails were too uniform to be hand wrought. He was about to close the lid when he saw the label.

"What does the label have on it?" he asked.

"Label? Why, Sister, did you know that the old chest actually has a label in it?"

"How interesting," Miriam remarked, as she bent over to look at it, as if she had never seen it before. "Here, let me move some of this old stuff so we can read it better."

Mr. Zimmerman was helping straighten up the contents of the box when he noticed their so-called picnic ware.

I better tread softly, he thought to himself, for this may be another hoax. But there they were — a tall stack of twelve-inch flat pewter plates with eagle touch-marks. There were also a large pewter pitcher, two bowls, and at least five porringers. He did not dare pick up the pitcher or examine the porringers for fear of disclosing his interest before the watchful eyes of the shrewd ladies. Quickly he calculated that there was at least a thousand dollars worth of early American pewter among their picnic ware.

"If I were to buy your chest, what will you do with your picnic ware?"

"That will be a problem, since we've always kept it stored in the tea chest, but we will have to manage," replied Glenda.

"We seldom use it, now. Not that it is not still good, but our new set of Merrimac is so light and pretty," added Miriam.

"You ladies are fortunate to have two sets of picnic ware." Then, Mr. Zimmerman's face took on a studied look. "I was thinking . . . No. Three hundred dollars is really out of the question for me."

"You were considering buying the chest?" asked Glenda.

"Well, not really. My wife will have a birthday next week, and she does like American primitives, but I don't know what she would use a chest like that for. She doesn't have any picnic ware to store, and three hundred dollars is just more than I can spend on her gift."

"Sister, since it's for his wife's birthday, couldn't we let him have it for two-fifty?"

"I think we should and let him have the old picnic ware for her too."

Mr. Zimmerman's heart skipped a beat, and he had to wait a second to get his composure. "You ladies are so very kind and generous, but I'm afraid I'll have to refuse your offer. I love my wife very much, but you see, two hundred dollars is all that I can spend on her birthday this year."

"Two hundred?" pondered Miriam.

"Yes, I'm sorry that I can't get this for her. I know she would just love it." Mr. Zimmerman closed the lid and gave the chest an affectionate pat.

"Well," Miriam started.

"No, no," Mr Zimmerman interrupted. "I can't ask you ladies to part with such a valuable piece of Americana for a mere two hundred dollars."

"We insist," both said in unison.

"Nothing will make us happier than helping to make your wife's birthday one to remember," Miriam added.

"Since you put it that way, I'll pay you and get the chest and books out of your way."

As soon as the door was locked behind their first customer, Miriam waltzed around the room, waving the handful of bills. "Sister, that little memento paid off."

"Yes, but that young man was so naive and personable, I was tempted to exchange our pretty new Merrimac for that old picnic ware."

"We needed to do no more. Didn't you see the satisfaction that swathed him as he carted Papa's old kindling box out of here?"

"Yes. He looked as happy with that old box, excuse me, tea chest, as we are with our cash," said Glenda.

"Almost." Both ladies laughed.

"Glenda, that transaction proves your point — Ignorance is bliss."

**Telling time: 19-20 minutes**
**Audience: adult shoppers**

*Usually women enjoy this story more than anyone. But there are men who are shoppers too, and some will identify with one or more of the characters in the story even if they are not shoppers. It is a worthy story for the teller's repertoire.*

# Index of Places and Names

If you enjoyed this book, here are some other books from Pineapple Press on related topics. For a complete catalog, write to Pineapple Press, P.O. Box 3899, Sarasota, FL 34230, or call (800) 746-3275.

## History/Biography/Folklore

*Classic Cracker* by Ronald W. Haase. A study of Florida's wood-frame vernacular architecture that traces the historical development of the regional building style that offered human comfort in Florida's environment.

*Dreamers, Schemers and Scalawags: The Florida Chronicles, Vol. 1* by Stuart B. McIver. Engaging character sketches of unusual characters who made Florida their home: includes storytellers, tycoons, moviemakers, and more.

*Florida Place Names* by Allen Morris. A unique reference that describes the origin and meaning of the name of every county and incorporated city in Florida as well as hundreds of others. Includes a hundred black and white photos edited by Joan Perry Morris, curator of the Florida State Archives.

*Florida's Past* (3 volumes) by Gene Burnett. A popular collection of essays about the people and events that shaped the state.

*Legends of the Seminoles* by Betty Mae Jumper with Peter Gallagher. Tales told around the campfires to Seminole children, now written down for the first time. Each story illustrated with an original painting by Guy LaBree.

*Murder in the Tropics: The Florida Chronicles, Vol. 2* by Stuart McIver. A compelling collection of true crime in paradise.

## Historical Fiction

*A Land Remembered* by Patrick Smith. A sweeping saga of three generations of Florida settlers. Winner of the Florida Historical Society's Tebeau Prize as the Most Outstanding Florida Historical Novel.

*Guns of the Palmetto Plains* by Rick Tonyan. An action-packed Cracker Western that plunges the reader into the last agonizing years of the Civil War. Snake-filled swamps, Yankee raiders, and vicious outlaws block the trails between Florida and the rest of the Confederacy, leaving the untamed peninsula to the heroes and the gunslingers.

*Riders of the Suwannee* by Lee Gramling. Tate Barkley returns to Florida in the 1870s from the Western frontier, only to find out that his gunfighting days are not over. When Tate pulls out his Winchester, you can count on the kind of action that will keep pages turning right on to the all-out fight at the end of this Cracker Western.

*Thunder on the St. Johns* by Lee Gramling. The vast unsettled lands of Florida in the 1850s are home to honest hard-working homesteaders and greedy violent power mongers. Which kind of folk will prevail in this gripping Cracker Western?

*Trail from St. Augustine* by Lee Gramling. In this Cracker Western a fur trapper and a young woman are pursued across the Florida wilderness to a showdown on the windswept sands of the Florida Gulf coast.

oven. His auntie gave Epaminondas several slices while it was still warm, and then she gave him a nice, big, crusty loaf to take home for him and his mammy.

Epaminondas remembered exactly what his mammy told him. He reached deep into his pocket and got out a ball of string. He tied one end of the string around the loaf of bread and just led it along home.

When his mammy saw him, she asked, "Epaminondas, what are ya 'pose to be draggin' 'hind you?"

"Bread, Mammy, Auntie sent ya a big nice loaf of her bread."

Mammy sighed a deep sigh. "Epaminondas, ya ain't got the sense ya wus born with. Ya ain't never had the sense ya wus born with, and you never goin' ter have the sense ya wus born with. And I'm tired of tellin' ya how to truck. Ya jest stay home, and I'll go to Auntie's."

A few days later, Mammy got her bonnet and her shawl. She put her basket on her arm, and walked to the front gate. "Epaminondas," she called, "I'm goin' to Auntie's, to take her one of my mulberry pies. And I want you to stay home."

"I'd sure lak ter go."

"I won't be gone long, and I want ye to stay here. I've got three more mulberry pies coolin' on the steps; so, be careful how ya step on them. Keep the flies and chickens off of the pies till I get back."

"Yessum."

Epaminondas kept the flies and chickens shewed away from the pies while they were cooling, and then he got to thinking about what his Mammy had said — to "be careful how he stepped on them"; so, he decided that he'd better step right on the middle of each one of those pies, and that was exactly what he did.

I don't know the ending to this story, for no one has ever told me the ending, but I bet you can end it, for me, can't you?

**Telling time: 10-12 minutes**
**Audience: pre-school - adult**

*Everyone enjoys "Epaminondas." There are a number of variations — talking animals, Chinese, and Appalachian Jack to name a few. But the original is my favorite, and judging from the laughter of the audience, it is also the favorite of many. The best assurance to avoid seeming to be poking fun at some race or culture is to make Epaminondas a member of your culture. Everyone, even small children and grown men, are amused at being able to be a jump ahead of the teller in this story. Easy to learn, fun to tell, always a crowd pleaser, "Epaminondas" is a story which I have been telling for more than sixty years and still get numerous requests to tell.*

# Gator Tadd
# or
# How the Green Swamp Got Its Name

**A** **number of years back** — a hundred to be more specific — there lived, in Jacksonville, a man who stood seven feet, eight inches tall and weighed more than three hundred pounds, named Sir Thadious Abelard deDiare. In spite of his distinguished name, his unusual size, and his outstanding artistic ability, everyone called him "Gator Tadd."

Can't say for sure whether or not he was a native. Some said he was, and others said he just drifted down here looking for warm weather, where his paint wouldn't freeze. This might have been so, for he was a master painter and made all his paint from his own secret recipe.

Gator Tadd did some impressive jobs around Jacksonville. He painted all the insurance companies' high-rise buildings. He did them fast and right. With his twenty-five-gallon bucket in one hand and his twenty-five-inch brush in the other, there just wasn't a job too big for him to tackle.

He said, "If there ever was a crime 'gainst nature, it's this way they've got here of late of blowin' paint on with a spray gun, like they're tryin' to kill cockroaches, skeeters, or sandfleas."

Gator Tadd like to slap his paint on with a good twelve-inch brush, and he was never known to leave a run, a sag, a brush-lap, or a brush-bristle on the surface. Whether he slapped it on up and down, crosswise, or antigogglin', when Gator Tadd finished a job, the paint was as smooth as melting ice.

Gator Tadd never had a helper. He really didn't need one, for he could get himself up the side of a building as quick as a monkey can shin up a palm tree. If he needed anything on the ground, he just flipped it up to where he was working with his drag. (For any of you who are uninformed on the Cracker arts, a drag is a cow whip.)

Gator Tadd enjoyed an audience when he was working and for some time he had one, but there just weren't as many people around then, and his antics became "old hat." People quit coming around to watch, and so he lost interest in painting buildings.

He decided to take up signboard painting. He erected a hundred-foot signboard on the south bank of the St. Johns River and started soliciting the Jacksonville merchants for business. He promised them that he'd make the sign so real and true to life that no one would have to read it to get the message. That was a big selling point, for the merchants knew that there were many people with money to spend who could not read.

His first customer was The Tender Tasty Meat Market. He painted the letters they wanted on his signboard, and then he added some big juicy T-bone steaks. Those steaks looked so natural that the gators started attacking the signboard. Gator Tadd knew he had to do something about that. He looked over the entire herd, picked out the best-looking girl gator, put a bridle on her, and rode her back into Alligator Creek, and you know every one of those bull gators followed her. (Folks who saw him do this figured that such antics was how he got his name.) But the gators kept coming back, and soon the owners of the ocean liners, which brought visitors to Florida, started complaining that the gators were scaring the tourists away; so, the chamber of commerce made Gator Tadd remove the steaks.

Later he got a job painting the signboard for The Sunshine Bakery. Gator Tadd painted the words they wanted and a big loaf of bread. He painted it so well that every morning, when the sun hit that signboard, you could smell that bread baking. And if you looked at it, your stomach started rubbing a blister on your backbone. Some birds pecked at that picture until they wore their bills off and starved to death, because they didn't have anything left to peck with. Others just sat there — perched on the top of the billboard — trying to figure out the problem till they just keeled over. Either way, it was death to birds. The Audubon Society complained so much that Gator Tadd had to paint the loaf out.

These two incidents got people afraid to hire Gator Tadd, even though the butcher and the baker were doing a whopping business.

Finally, The Hot Ziggedy Thermonuclear Heater and Range Company hired him to do a sign for their new heater. Gator Tadd painted the heater with a fire going good inside and heat pouring off in every direction. I guess that in some ways it was the best job Gator Tadd ever did. During the coldest winter ever recorded by the Weather Bureau, on the first day of January, the dandelions and phlox started blooming in the little plot between the billboard and the river.

It was when the bums and river rats started making the place a hang-out that the citizens and storekeepers in the neighborhood put up a howl. The hobos drove nails into the billboard so they could hang kettles and cans on the top of the heater. That way they could cook their food and heat water to shave. And they found it more comfortable on the ground in front of that heater than in any flophouse in the city so they slept there, too.

Finally, the company came up with the idea of having Gator Tadd make the heater a lot hotter to drive the bums and river rats away. So he did. He changed the stove from a fiery red to a white hot, and made the heat waves a lot thicker. This drove all the bums across the river, but it also blistered the paint on all the boats in the river. Then, one day, a boathouse began to smoke, and then to blaze. The insurance companies faxed an ultimatum to the Hot Ziggedy Thermonuclear Heater and Range Company to jerk that billboard down and be quick about it, or they'd take them to court.

Now, uninformed historians have falsely accused Gator Tadd of starting that great Jacksonville fire that destroyed more than two thousand buildings on May 3, 1901. But Gator Tadd's signboard had been torn down and doused in the St. Johns River a full month before that fateful Friday when flames left the entire city a charred, gruesome specter.

After the fire, Gator Tadd packed his satchel and moved south to Orlando.

In Orlando, Gator Tadd perfected his own special type of skywriting. His signs didn't fade away in a minute like the smoke that pours out of a plane and gets torn to pieces by the wind before you can hardly spell out what it says. He got lots of jobs advertising on the sky. It was all pretty and fancy colors, and it'd stay right there for days if the weather was fair. Of course, birds would fly through it, and when it'd rain the colors would all run together, and then, when the clouds rolled by, there'd be what folks got to callin' a rainbow. It really was nothing but Gator Tadd's skywriting all jumbled together.

Nobody never did understand how Gator Tadd managed to do his sky painting. When people asked him, he'd say, "That's for me to know and you to find out." And it seems that no one ever found out. But this much is known:

Between Orlando and Tampa is a whole bunch of lakes, marshes, and woods which cover about nine hundred square miles or 576,000 acres. When Gator Tadd came to Orlando this area was known as "the swamp." It was in the middle of this swamp that Gator Tadd rented a thou-